What Have You Got In Your Bag?

Stories of an Irish Aid Worker

Theresa McDonnell Friström

6tHouse

First published in 2012 by
6tHouse
an imprint of Wordsonthestreet
Six San Antonio Park,
Salthill,
Galway, Ireland.
web: www.wordsonthestreet.com
email: publisher@wordsonthestreet.com

The moral right of the author has been asserted.
A catalogue record for this book is available from the British Library.

ISBN   978-1-907017-14-8

Cover design, layout and typesetting: Wordsonthestreet
Cover image: Theresa McDonnell Friström
Printed and bound in the UK

What Have You Got In Your Bag?

Pamela,
with best wishes!
Theresa

To Gunnar

ABOUT THE AUTHOR

Theresa McDonnell Friström is a former International Development Worker. She worked in management positions for Concern Worldwide in Asia and Africa, for Irish Aid, Government of Ireland, in Uganda and South Africa, and for Vita (RTI International) Dublin.

She holds an M.Sc. (Econ) from Swansea University, Wales and Diplomas in Social Policy and Administration (Swansea University), Human Resource Management (IMI/Trinity College Dublin), and Disaster Management (Dhaka University, Bangladesh).
She has researched Social Performance Management in Microfinance at University College Dublin and studied Swedish at Lund University.

She began her overseas development work as a volunteer with Concern in Bangladesh (1973-75) and continued to work with Concern over the following twenty years, as Assistant Country Director in Thailand (1979/80), Country Director in Uganda (1981/82), Tanzania (1982/83), Sudan (1984), Bangladesh (1988/89), as Head of a number of Departments, and Member of Emergency Teams in Dublin (up to 1994). She was the first female Head of Personnel Division (in 1992), was Country Director in Cambodia for three years (2002/05), and was the first Chairperson of the Board of AMK Cambodia (2003-2005).

She was the second Programme Officer appointed by Irish Aid in Uganda (1994/99) and in South Africa in 2000. She worked with Vita in Dublin as Programme Advisor, primarily for Ethiopia, for two and a half years, (2005/08)

She is a Member of Concern, a Member of the CLTS Foundation, and an Associate Medical Missionary of Mary (AMMM).

She currently teaches English in Simrishamns Komun, Sweden.

She was born and grew up in Rathcoole, Co. Dublin, Ireland and is married to Gunnar Friström. She now divides her time between Ireland and Sweden.

CONTENTS

Acknowledgements

I would like to thank everyone who helped to create these stories. You are too many to mention by name, but without you, there would be no stories. I hope you enjoy reminiscing.

I want to acknowledge my gratitude to the late Father Aengus Finucane, C.S.Sp, for all I learned from and with him while he was my boss, my mentor, and my friend over many decades.

I owe a special thank-you to my husband, Gunnar, to my *"Språkmorska" (my special name for* my Swedish language teacher in Brantevik), Birgitta Mattson, and her husband Professor Jan Thavenius for reading my stories and for their encouragement to continue.

I want to thank my writing teacher, David Rice, and my fellow learners at the Killaloe Hedge School for Writers, for their encouragement to write.
I want to thank Writers Literary Agency and my editor Laura Monroe for all their valuable advice.

And finally, I want to thank all of you who buy this book and encourage your friends to buy it as well!

INTRODUCTION

She read somewhere that all good things come in threes.

About herself, she says:

1. She was a happy child and enjoyed running around in her bare feet regardless of the season or weather. But she was shy. She blushed and even tried to hide when anyone spoke to her or disturbed her dreaming. She was introduced early in life to dance and drama. She remembers her first speaking role in the local drama group. It was Maisie Madigan in Seán O'Casey's *Juno and the Paycock*. She remembers this as a turning point in her life, as it allowed her to enjoy playing in the limelight. But even now she is happy in the background, and the way she tells her stories in the third person seems just right for her.

2. She was a fixer, a dreamer, and an optimist who didn't become cynical. Some say this made her unusual. She believed that it was possible to make a difference and she was always more likely to act on behalf of others - others who were weaker, smaller, less able to take care of themselves - rather than to fix things for herself. She didn't forget her mother's advice: "If you're big, be merciful."

3. She was always interested in travel. The first essay she remembers writing was on travel and she wrote about Bianconi's cars. Many of the stories that followed were written while she travelled on trains and aeroplanes, and while she waited at railway stations and airports.

About the stories, she says:

1. They don't appear in official reports, job descriptions, or white papers, but they want to be told.

2. They tell of what happened when other things were planned - what some people call life.

3. She thinks of them as the "extras" in a life's work and hopes that, as water drops separate from a great mass and play in the sunshine, they may brighten a day like a rainbow!

CHAPTER 1

WHAT'S IN YOUR BAG?

"What's in your bag?" she asked the little one who met them at the door.

"My things," the little one replied.

The little one loved bags. She loved to have them, to investigate what was in them, to organise them, to pack them, to unpack them, to carry them, to show them off.

"This is where I live now," the little one said as she led them into the living room. "And today you are our guests."

They had come together for a housewarming party - a party for the little one's parents' aunties and uncles. They were many, but the house was not crowded. This was good because, although it was a fine evening in late June, it was not warm enough to sit outside.

The living room was furnished with two generous sofas, a couple of armchairs, and a large, low glass-topped table that stood on a rug in the centre of the floor. The fireplace was open and as yet unfinished. The furniture was dark, but the room was bright. The walls were painted in a plain off-white, and the window was full-length and almost the width of one wall. It looked out over the wide expanse of fields and rolling hills of Upper Punchestown in Co. Kildare.

The little one was dressed in her new red and white gingham dress with matching red crochet bodice that her granny had made for her. She wore her first pair of shoes with heels, and she carried the new bag that her other granny had given her over her arm. She proudly walked around - tottering on her heels sometimes - carrying a big plate with small pieces of grilled rabbit, which she offered to her guests.

"Would you like some rabbit?" the little one asked, often adding, "What have you got in your bag?"

"Mind!" someone called. "The rabbit's going to fall."

The little one moved around the room with the big plate.

"Be careful!" someone else called.

"Would you like some rabbit?" the little one asked her grand-aunt, then added, "Your bag is very small – what have you got in it?"

The little one put the big plate down on the low table. As she did so, her new bag slid down her arm and hit the side of the table. Almost all of the little pieces of grilled rabbit slid onto the glass. Without giving it a second glance, the little one settled herself on the rug beside her grand-aunt.

"Your bag is very small," she said again. "Can I look?" Then she continued, "You know, you're not allowed to root in other people's bags."

As she said this, the little one's fingers moved to open the little black bag. "What have you got in it?"

"I have all my important things," her grand-aunt answered.

The little one's blue eyes opened wide. "How could all your *im-port-ant* things fit in that little bag?" she asked, with emphasis.

"Okay, I'll show you," her grand-aunt answered as the little one opened the bag, and together they started to take everything out.

"This is the key to my flat," her grand-aunt said. "These are my cards and –"

"What do you do with all your cards?" the little one interrupted.

"This one," her grand-aunt said, "is to get money from the bank; this one is my driving licence; this is for flying on an aeroplane; this one is for the train or bus . . ."

"I have no cards," the little one said sadly.

"You will when you're big," her grand-aunt comforted her.

"What's this little thing?" the little one asked. "And this?"

"This is my money purse," replied her grand-aunt. "It's from Laponia. This is my telephone, and my address book is in there, too. This is my lip gloss."

"I know what this is," the little one said as she took out the camera and lined it up on the glass table top beside all the other things that had come out of the little black bag. "But what is this little thing?" she asked.

"That's my memory stick," her grand-aunt answered.

"What's a memory stick?" the little one asked.

Suddenly, there was a call from the other room. "Where's the rabbit?" It was the one who had organised the rabbit for this special occasion.

"It's here on the table," the little one called back without even turning her head. Then she continued to ask her grand-aunt: "What do you do with a *mem-o-ry* stick?"

"I use it to save all my stories," her grand-aunt answered. "I save them here so that I won't lose them."

"All what stories?" the little one asked.

"Stories from my life and many of them are from Africa," her grand-aunt answered.

"Can I see your stories?" the little one asked.

"You can when I print them," her grand-aunt answered.

"Well, when are you going to print them, then?" the little one asked.

Before she could answer, they were called to the table for dinner. As the grand-aunt put everything back into her bag, the little one noticed another interesting bag, got to her feet, stumbled over her new heels, and followed the bag.

As the grand-aunt marvelled at the little one's curiosity, she remembered a story the little one's mother told a week earlier about a visit to the little one's favourite shop. The little one said it was her favourite shop because she liked the colours - the reds, greens, oranges, yellows - of the fruits and vegetables. She said she liked the smells too, even if she was unsure about the smell of oranges. And, of course, she was interested in the people and what they had in their bags.

As was her way, the little one wandered around the shop, careful not to disturb the pyramids of apples, oranges, pears, potatoes, beetroots, cabbages, and cauliflowers that the shopkeeper had arranged. As she went, she looked around to see who was there that she might talk to.

The shopkeeper was fascinated by her conversations.

"What's your name?" he asked the little one when she came near.

"Rosie," the little one answered.

"What age are you, Rosie?" the shopkeeper asked her.

"I'm four, and do you know what my favourite food is now?" the little one asked. Without waiting for his reply, she continued, "It's broccoli and it's good for me."

"Will you come back here when you're sixteen?" the shopkeeper asked her. "I'll give you a job."

The little one looked puzzled. Then she said, "I can't. I'm going to be a doctor."

"Well, come in here while you're studying," he said, "and I'll give you a job."

"Okay, I'll think about it," the little one said.

Soon, everyone was seated around the three tables that the little one had helped to set for the dinner, and the first course -

a tasty and light vegetable soup - was served.

During dinner, the little one continued to investigate what people had in their bags. Suddenly, from across the room, the great-aunt heard the little one's voice: "Theresa McDonnell says she has stories in her bag, on a *mem-o-ry* stick, and that she's going to put them in a book. Did you ever hear anything so stupid?"

Other voices echoed around the table:

"Are we in it?"

"Are we in the stories?"

"Am I in it?"

"If Claudia's in it, then I want to be in it, too . . ."

CHAPTER 2

THE FIRST RAINBOW

These stories begin in Ireland in a cold winter in November 1947. There's not much that she remembers about the beginning. She used to wonder why - in fact, she used to ask why - about almost everything. Now she's content to let the memories flow as they will, gently or chaotically, in waves or as individual drops.

She's sitting in their lovely sandy garden in Brantevik, Sweden, looking out over the Baltic Sea, grateful that the wind has stopped blowing in from the east. There is almost no sound. Her mind wanders, becomes one with the gentle swell, and memories gather.

First, she remembers smells from her childhood: the welcome aroma of freshly baked bread, chocolate, new tar confirming summertime, freshly mown hay, freshly cut grass, wallflowers, Nivea cream, horses. She notes that her appreciation for the wonderful aromas of freshly ground coffee and chicken frying in butter with pepper and salt came later.

There's a scene she remembers. She's three years old (it's around her third birthday) and she's standing in her mother's bedroom, near the window with the white lace curtain that blocks the view to the front garden and out to the road, beside the dark wood dressing table with the big swinging mirrors. She is fascinated by these mirrors, by how she can look in one and see the sides and the back of her head and her long dark plaits in another. But now she's not looking in the mirror; she's looking up at her godmother who is giving her a pair of white socks for her birthday.

There's another scene where she's running around happily in her bare feet and she can hear herself laughing!

And now there's a little wave of memories.

She sees red toes in the wintertime.

There's a piece of four-inch-thick ice that has been taken from the water barrel near the back door, and she hears it breaking and sees it being set into the saddlebag of a bicycle.

There's the fine summer's day when they're all in the back playing. Each girl has a new dress and she's wondering what's wrong with aunties. Why do aunties dress little girls in new dresses and then send them outside to play? And then there is great excitement when they're called in and lined up to go into their mother's bedroom to see their new little brother.

It's a first day at school. He came with her because more children are needed to keep the three teachers, and he's allowed to sit at her desk in the big room because he's only three.

She sees her white First Communion dress being cut out of the wringers of the washing machine after its first wash.

She remembers seeing, with her first pair of glasses, the individual leaves on trees.

Now there's a bigger wave of memories: flooding on the eighth of December one year that stopped the annual shopping trip to Dublin; minding "the three little ones"; Irish dancing; chéilidhs and plays; a blue Volkswagen van; whist drives; national donkey derbies; bicycle races; a game called "three goals in" played across the road; horse-drawn hay bogies; after-dinner walks around the hill on Sunday afternoons and during school holidays; visitors; picnics and outings to the Japanese Gardens, the zoo, Blessington Lakes, and to the seaside at Donabate; snowballs; a tin bath; the water-mark in fine writing paper; stories with tears from Clady and Urney; knitting, sewing, crochet, gardening, and clipping hedges; painting and wallpaper; drama festivals, competitions, medals, and cups; driving lessons; a grey Cortina with a bench seat; camping; a blue Anniversary Beetle; a green Corolla.

She remembers watching raindrops running down the windowpane on a Sunday afternoon as the smell of vanilla wafted from the madeira cake baking in the top oven of the Aga cooker, while she sat at the kitchen table supposedly doing her homework. She sees in her mind's eye how the clouds drifted away, the sun peeped through, the play of light in the raindrops, and finally, the rainbow. She blinks and blinks again. She sees a rainbow out over the sea!

She remembers the busyness of preparing for and competing in rural drama festivals. She remembers the successes of their group in the 1972/73 competition season and how, in the midst of prizes and advancing to regional and national competitions, Bangladesh suddenly entered her life in early 1973.

It was in Bangladesh that she began to learn about extremes.

There is so much that could be said about Bangladesh: a country with a landmass that is one and a half times as big as Ireland, her home country, with a population estimated in 1973 to be 73 million people and in 2010 to be 150 million people. The most Ireland could ever claim was 8 million before the great famine of 1845–47, and 3 to 5 million since then.

She remembers writing home soon after her arrival in Bangladesh about how the pre-departure films and talks had prepared her for almost everything, except the smells. Now she can't recall those smells, but she remembers that their impact was great.

In Bangladesh in December 2010 (she was there with a

group of friends and former colleagues to celebrate a wedding), she saw herself as one of those old people from her childhood who loved to talk about things they remembered from thirty or forty years earlier. She marvelled at how time passes, how things change, and yet how things remain the same.

She remembers the shock in 2002 when she didn't recognise Dhanmondi, the part of Dhaka where she lived and worked for three years in the early 1970s and two years in the late 1980s. The "big house" that was such a part of her life then is almost the only building from her memory of Dhanmondi that still remains. All the other one- or two-storey houses have been knocked down and replaced by six- or seven-storey apartment buildings with about three metres between them.

Standing in the big room at the end of the corridor in the big house, the memories roll forward like a series of waves. She remembers the thunderstorm of her first night; the agony of a colleague in a nearby bed who was badly sunburned; the big round dining table and the great meals they shared; late-night parties with sing-songs and recitations, especially "The Green Eye of the Little Yellow God" and "If I Were a Lady"; early mornings and late nights of work and planning; and the crochet wedding dress that was burned to the bottom of a pot.

She remembers the coffin that was delivered one month before the death of their wonderful and beautiful colleague, Sr. Dr. Elizabeth O'Brien. She remembers sitting on the roof after Liz's funeral (because Liz didn't want any tears at her funeral) watching a most wonderful rainbow.

She remembers standing and then sitting in the crowded offices of the Central Bank, watching the men who sat behind very big desks - the people who tried to hand over at least three telephones while one spoke into another and the piles of files that were passed in front, one at a time, with open pages for signature, and then how they were effortlessly tossed to another pile on the floor on the other side of the big desks. Finally, after a very long time, it was her turn and her paper was signed: the paper that would allow them to use foreign exchange to buy food for distribution to victims of the 1974 floods. When she returned to her office, someone said, "You were a long time!"

In 2010, they walked through the rest of the house. It was being used now as a fitness centre, but otherwise it was unchanged. They stood for a moment's silence in the tiny room that had been the Big Man's room - the man who was her first boss in Bangladesh, her boss in different roles for over two decades, her mentor, and her friend until his death in 2009.

In the way that a huge wave can change a landscape forever and yet not leave individual traces, she is aware of how much Bangladesh impacted and influenced the rest of her working life. But it didn't happen all at once.

She remembers standing at Dhaka airport about three months after her arrival in 1973 and thinking that if she could have just one wish fulfilled, it would be to take a direct flight from Dhaka to Rathcoole. Then she would promise never to ask to go anywhere ever again!

There is one strong feeling she carries from Bangladesh. If she allows herself one "hate" today, it is poverty. She knows that poverty is not static and not one-dimensional - and she can still hear Mother Teresa saying, when they met her in Calcutta in the early 1970s, that, "The poverty of spirit in the Western world is every bit as corrosive as the physical poverty people suffer in the Indian subcontinent or anywhere else in the world." She is aware that great adversity can bring about great creativity. It is the destructive nature of poverty that she hates.

She remembers the first time she had an inkling of what having nothing really meant. It was in Bangladesh - Dhaka, Khulna, Chittagong, and other cities - in late 1974 and early 1975 when thousands of people who had lost the last of their meagre possessions and their land in the floods of 1974 moved into the cities and towns. She remembers how the settlements in the centre of the roads expanded, as there was nowhere else for people to go; how those people, especially women with small children, had nothing except what they carried on their bodies or in their arms; and how, during one week in early 1975, those streets were cleared as the people were piled into trucks and driven out of the cities and towns to new "settlement" sites where they were unloaded and left with equally nothing.

She feels these thoughts drawing her attention far away into, as she sees in her mind's eye, a deep pit. It is dark at the bottom. There the destructive nature of poverty is playing side by side with the destructive nature of wealth, power, and greed. She watches for a while, and as the vision fades, she hears a voice asking, "What will be the outcome for a world of broken promises?"

She shakes her head. The rainbow is gone now, the sky is clear, and the sea is reflecting a deep blue.

There is another wave of memories. Her memory is drawn back to 1988 when three-quarters of Bangladesh was under water. She was in awe of those big rivers that flowed into the eastern and western sides of Bangladesh, especially when she learned that it was only the last 8 percent or so of their long journey from the Himalayas to the Bay of Bengal that flowed through Bangladesh. She understood that there was normally about four weeks between the peaking of the rivers, but in late August and early September 1988 the great rivers peaked at the same time and this coincided with a high tide in the Bay of

Bengal. She remembers their colleagues in Saidpur making a collection to support the flood relief effort, grateful for once that their little part of the country was not affected. She remembers the volunteers - people who couldn't go to their own jobs because of the floods - who arrived at their office and houses in Dhanmondi to help with the emergency food distributions.

She remembers the cooking pots that filled the backyard and the smoke that filled the whole office, causing tears to stream down their faces as they worked late into the night with people whose own office was flooded to complete agreements for co-funding so that their flood relief work could continue in the morning.

She remembers the boat journeys when the engine broke down and they had to row with their hands through the night, as well as the concrete tubewell platforms standing 15 metres up in the air that were - along with broken bits of pottery scattered here and there in the mud - the silent and only physical evidence of where the ground had been before the flood.

She remembers the great change in the landscape of the tea garden in Jaflong when the river changed its course and knocked down the only brick-built school in the area. She remembers with special pride her great team of co-workers and how together they accomplished in two short years what could ordinarily be about ten years of work.

Thinking of the creativity and resourcefulness of the Bangladeshi people, her memory wanders to Jordan in the early 1990s. She recalls the lights in only one part of the refugee camps for migrant workers who fled from the Iraq/Kuwait War and the strange feeling of pride she felt when she discovered that it was the Bangladeshi section. Everybody in the camps had been given the same rations, but the Bangladeshis were the only ones who ate the fish from the cans and used the leftovers to make oil lamps.

Her gaze is far out over the sea. Thinking of refugee camps draws a new wave of memories, this time from Thailand.

She remembers that it was in Thailand in 1979–80, in camps for people who fled wars in Laos, Vietnam, and Cambodia, that she first learned about man-made disasters.

In her memory, she can still hear the deep silence in a camp with about 25,000 people who had recently escaped from a Khmer Rouge–controlled area. In another camp she can still see the faces of the refugees who had fled from the Khmer Rouge five years earlier - the fear in their eyes when they saw that the new arrivals who would now become their near neighbours were their old "enemy," recent refugees from the Khmer Rouge who still wore the Khmer Rouge black shirts and trousers.

She remembers the strict control that was exercised over access to and from the camps and the bonfires along the road, where everything unauthorised was burned. And she remembers plastic - bottles, basins, plates, mugs, and cutlery; plastic in all colours, plastic in all shapes; plastic in all sizes; plastic everything it seemed - and how it was loved!

From Thailand, she moved to Uganda.

She detects a change in her memories. There is a separation. Stories are emerging, separating from the waves of memories just as gemstones separate from rocks. These are stories that want to be told.

She sees a collection of stories now as she envisions in her mind's eye the drops of water that separate from the great mass of the River Nile. The drops spray over the narrow gap at Murchison Falls, play and dance in the sunshine with the light, and create a wonderful rainbow before tumbling down to rejoin the river on its long journey through Uganda, Sudan, and Egypt.

She feels the separation, too, as she remembers the feeling of separating individual stitches when she helped her mother to rip a knitted dress and use the blue and cream Aran wool to crochet a wonderful bedspread.

She imagines the separation as part of a timeless process of creative unravelling and renewal: the one and the whole.

CHAPTER 3

PANETTONE

T he man put down the telephone and said: "He said he'll be here in five minutes."

It was late and they all knew it. If they didn't leave soon, they would not make it to the border that day. Even as it was, they may not make it, and none of them wanted that. It was so much extra trouble to have to book into a hotel for the night.

The border closed at 6:00 p.m. and they should really arrive there before 5:00 p.m. because of the procedures to be followed for exporting the car from Kenya and importing it into Uganda. They were quite familiar with the routines and knew that they worked well but at times could be slow because of the amount of traffic.

"Should we postpone the trip until tomorrow?" someone asked.

Without hesitation, the answer was, "No, not if we can help it."

They were in Nairobi in the house that acted as a base for their programme in Karamoja in northeastern Uganda. Somebody had to make this trip every five or six weeks to keep the team in Uganda supplied for their programmes and for themselves. It was the early 1980s, when there was not much that could be bought in Uganda.

As they stood calculating the minutes it would take for this and that, a car drove in the gate. The driver jumped out and went to the back of his car. They ran out and opened the boot of their car.

"I'm sorry I'm late," he said as he lifted a big box from his boot. "This should be all you need." He tried to fit the box into their car.

They had to take out a few bags and then repack them around the big cardboard box.

"I think that will do now," he said when he was satisfied with the packing. "Have a safe trip and see you soon again."

With that, he jumped back into his car, reversed out the gate, and was gone.

They collected their handbags, got into their car, and reversed out.

It took them about an hour to get out of the city, and then they were on the highway leading northwest through Nakuru, Kisumu, and Kakamega, to the border posts at Busia.

It was a nice route along the Rift Valley. The road was reasonably good - it was very good in some places, but in others, where the tarred surface had broken up, there were deep and sharp-edged potholes. These could be very difficult for the car and for the passengers, especially when one drove into them unexpectedly.

Their car was okay.

It was yellow, she remembers, but what make? No, she can't remember - and she used to be good with cars!

It was comfortable enough, but she didn't like driving it anymore. She had a feeling that the back didn't exactly follow the front. This, she knew, was a difficult explanation, but she couldn't think of how else to describe the feeling she had with the steering. She thought that maybe the underside had hit a few too many of the sharp-edged potholes.

The weather was okay - a little overcast, no rain, not too hot, not too cold in the higher areas, and no mist either - and they made good progress. They had agreed to not stop for food, drink, or anything else if they could avoid it, except to change drivers. This all worked well on that day.

At 4:55 p.m., they arrived and took their place in the queue at the Busia border crossing point. Someone got out and went to collect the various forms that had to be filled in for the car and for passport control for themselves. In their turn, they came to the desk. She can still recall the sound of the stamps and the rhythm as they first hit the inkpad and then the relevant papers. In time, all their papers were signed and stamped, and they were told to proceed with their car to customs for verification.

They joined the short queue at the customs post and waited their turn. When called forward, they drove up and stopped outside the building as was the routine. A young officer in a blue short-sleeved uniform shirt came, checked their papers, and asked them to open the boot. They had hoped to avoid the latter, as sometimes happened, but when asked they had to comply. This officer seemed to be interested in everything. One by one they answered his questions about what was in each bag. Then he asked what was in the brown cardboard box.

It was for one of their water projects, but exactly what was in the box none of them knew. He wasn't satisfied with their answers, so he asked them to open it, he wanted to see for himself what as in there.

It took a few minutes for them to get something to cut the tape, and then it was opened. He looked at the pieces of pipe, nuts, joints, bolts, and so forth, and asked what each one was for. All they could answer was that these materials were for a water project, that their colleague in Uganda was an engineer, not them, and they were just carrying the parts for him.

The officer asked to see their export permit.

"Have you got it?" they asked each other.

One rummaged in her bag, which was full of papers and much else, while another looked in her briefcase.

The officer in the blue short-sleeved shirt said he would have to call his boss. He asked them to wait where they were, and he disappeared into the building.

They stood, looking after him, looking at each other, looking at their watches, looking into the boot.

One of them noticed the Panettone box and realised she was hungry.

She hadn't known about Panettone, the Italian Christmas cake, before coming to work in Uganda, but now she was very familiar with it since the Italian sisters at the missions in Karamoja were very generous in sharing the supplies they got on a regular basis from their big benefactor, who came with a full container every six months or so. Panettone was now one of her favourite picnic foods for these long journeys because it was always fresh, moist, and tasty, and it had a wonderful aroma.

"Would anybody like some Panettone?" she asked. "We haven't had any lunch, and this could be as good time as any to have our picnic."

"Yes, please," they answered.

Soon they were standing around the open boot drinking cups of warm coffee and eating big pieces of Panettone, while those wonderful aromas wafted around them. As she savoured the tastes and the smells, she noticed a man standing a little way off, looking in their direction.

"Would you like some Panettone?" she asked him, thinking he must like these smells, too.

"Yes, please," he replied.

He seems to know Panettone, too, she thought as she cut

him a piece and someone else got a cup and poured him some coffee. He didn't talk much. In fact, she doesn't remember that he spoke at all, except to say thank you.

He ate his piece of Panettone, had another one, drank his coffee, and then left.

"Anybody like more Panettone?" she asked. "Anybody for more coffee?"

When they were finished, they packed their cups and flask, and the empty Panettone box away. "Panettone is wonderful for picnics," someone said, echoing her thoughts. "It stays so moist and the aroma is great."

By now they were anxiously looking at their watches. If they didn't go soon, they would be stuck for the night between the two border crossing points - in no-man's-land!

"Where is the one to check our car?" they asked another man in a blue short-sleeved shirt who passed by. He said he would check and went into the building.

He came back after just a few minutes and said: "He is the one who was here. He says you can go."

"Is he the one with whom we shared the Panettone?" They wondered as they looked at him and at each other but could say nothing but "thank you."

They closed the box, their bags, and the boot, climbed into the car, drove to the Ugandan border checkpoint, and filled in the papers as quickly as they could.

When they were clear of the border on the road to Iganga, they suddenly started to breathe normally, with a great sense of freedom that they would be home in Mbale within an hour.

One said: "If we tried to bribe someone, we couldn't have done it."

Many years later, after what had become an annual Christmas visit to their favourite Irish bookshop, Abtree, they went next door to their favourite supermarket, Superquinn, in Lucan. As they walked towards the cheese counter, she suddenly stopped and asked: "Where is the Panettone?" She hadn't seen it, but the aroma called to her, stopped her. It was the first time she had seen Panettone for sale in an Irish supermarket. She bought one, in remembrance of the Italian sisters and the men at the Busia border crossing point!

CHAPTER 4

IS THAT A SHOT?

"Is that a shot?" someone asked.

"There's another," someone said.

"Get down," someone yelled in a loud whisper.

"Oh shit, the light," someone said as they all lay flat on the ground, along with the overturned chairs, around the table.

Above the table, the one light - a long, bare fluorescent bulb - shone brightly down on them.

"We should turn off the light," someone said as more sounds of shots rang out in the near distance.

"Yes, we should turn off the light," someone replied, "but someone has to stand up to reach the switch, and who's going to do that?"

"It has to be someone with long legs and arms, so they can reach to it," someone whispered, and they all laughed a nervous laugh.

"There's more shooting, and it's getting closer. Someone please turn off the light; otherwise, we'll all be hit," someone pleaded.

"Okay, I'll do it," one of them said. He was tall. As he stood up, there was a rattling at their gate, voices called out, and there were more shots.

He hit the light switch and quickly fell back down to the ground, hitting a fallen chair. They all froze while he cursed under his breath. "I think I've wet myself," he said.

Now there was total confusion. Their gate burst open and a small truck without lights rolled into their dark yard.

The voices were clearer now.

"What way is this to welcome your neighbours on New Year's Eve?" they heard as people stepped out of the pickup, carrying bottles of champagne.

They lay silently and watched the unfolding scene. Slowly it dawned on them that there was no danger. The sounds were from firecrackers and not shot. One by one they got to their feet.

"How could you - "

"How could you?"

"How *could* you?"

The questions were never finished in the tumble of hugging, punching, laughing, and crying. Someone started to pick up the chairs; while someone else went to collect more glasses and someone else turned the light on again.

Soon they were all sitting around the table in the tookle (the round shelter with a thatched roof supported on wooden poles and half-walls made of bamboo) in the front yard of their small house in Namalu, southern Karamoja, in the northeast of Uganda, sipping the cool champagne.

"This has been one of the scariest moments in my life," one said.

"I don't think I'll ever be able to hear firecrackers again without thinking of shots," another added.

"Happy New Year 1982!" someone toasted.

"Happy New Year!" they all responded.

She had been in Uganda for about six months by then.

Six months, is that all? she wondered, as she reflected on all that had happened - so many new experiences. *Karamoja is a very special place*, she thought, remembering what she had read and heard about the region. Life was not easy, especially for the old, the young, the less able-bodied, or those without cattle.

"Cattle?" she remembers asking.

"Yes, cattle," her new colleague insisted, and then added: "People are dying with money in their fists. Nobody wants it; nobody can eat money."

"That's true everywhere. People can't eat money, but they can exchange it for food," another colleague responded.

31

"Well, this is different," the first colleague continued. "People here only value cattle. They believe they have a God-given right to all the cattle in the world and that others are only temporarily 'minding' them until they can 'go and collect them'. Now that the situation is normalising, the so-called 'working-class people' who have money and could afford to buy food are dying with the money in their fists because nobody wants it."

"What do you mean by 'working-class people'?" she asked.

"I mean people like teachers, police, administrators, nurses - all those who are paid in cash for their work," was the reply.

"What do you mean by 'the situation is normalising'?" another new colleague asked.

"I mean that the severe famine is over. Food distribution is working well, and people have more energy. The marriage season is approaching and people want to collect cattle to be able to pay a good bride price and therefore get a good wife for their sons and brothers," the first colleague said. "It simply means that cattle-raiding has started again, but a big difference this time is that raiders are using machine guns instead of the traditional spears. Raiding with spears was a test of skill, a test of manhood. With guns more people are killed or injured in the raids while not many cattle change hands. The simple fact is that the best-armed groups control most of the cattle - the wealth of the Karamojong."

"Yes," someone else added, "and those with guns but with no cattle - and no prospects or hopes of getting cattle - have turned their attention to raiding buses, cars, and jeeps. In fact, all vehicles travelling on these roads are now targets."

She remembers the lovely young Italian sister-nurse who was shot dead in one of those first "car raids," as they were called, as she drove back from a health meeting in Moroto about five months earlier. That was soon after her arrival, and she remembers how she wanted to leave this dangerous place then. She remembers clearly that her new colleagues who had been here a few months longer than her voted to stay. They argued that the famine was not over and the needs were greater than the risks. She felt she couldn't argue with this, so she agreed to stay, too.

She recalls how trying to weigh needs against risks had become a regular and common exercise over the months.

They were in a new growing season now. Programmes to distribute seeds had been successful, planting was widespread, and the rains had been good, but it wasn't yet time to harvest the crops.

"If we can hold out until the harvest is ready," everybody said, "then people have a fair chance of getting back on their feet and we can say we've done a good job."

And that was their aim. But the risks were increasing and, in tandem, their team was shrinking.

They had become used to the travel restrictions and worked hard to follow the recommendation to be close to home by 3:00 p.m. as everyone agreed that the risks of being shot, or shot at, seemed to be greater after 3:00 p.m.

This served them well for a couple of months. But now there was a change; now they were no longer safe in some houses.

They found this out the hard way when one of their houses was attacked on Christmas Eve. Fortunately, those who lived there were able to get out through a small window and run to the nearby police station, where they were able to spend the night. But they lost almost everything they had left in the house. Nobody would go to the house in the dark as they considered it to be too dangerous, and the raiders knew this. They knew that they had all the hours of darkness to take what they wanted.

All thoughts of Christmas celebrations went, as it were, out the window with the raid. Instead, their time was taken up in rescuing what was possible of their personal belongings and programme materials, in reviewing arrangements for the work they carried out in that area, and in re-negotiating agreements with local authorities and with international organisations in

Kampala.

The impact of the attack was great because foreign aid workers in general could no longer feel safe in their homes in Karamoja. After long discussions, there was general agreement that some places, such as Namalu, were still safe. It was also agreed that everybody should feel free to make up their own minds about staying, leaving, or being transferred. Those who decided that they were ready to leave Karamoja were transferred to programmes in other countries.

The people who agreed that Namalu was safe and that they wanted to stay were those who had assembled to celebrate New Year's Eve.

She wonders how much of this their neighbours and co-workers knew when they came to Namalu with their firecrackers and champagne bottles to celebrate New Year's 1982.

CHAPTER 5

I'D LIKE TO DRIVE YOUR CAR

I t was 6:00 p.m. and she was standing at the front door of their house in Mbale talking with Flora, their housekeeper, who was about to go home. It would be dark within an hour and Flora liked to be at home before dark.

Mbale was her home these days, even if she didn't spend much time there. It was centrally located, which means that it was a couple of hours drive from everywhere she needed to go for her work (mainly Karamoja, Kampala, and Nairobi), and the international telephone connection from the local post office to Ireland was good.

Their work permits for Uganda had just been renewed for five years - the woman in Kampala said it was easier that way because she didn't have any more application forms. So the regular six-month visits to that office would no longer be necessary.

She was happy to be back in Mbale and was looking forward to a couple of days' rest to unpack her bag, get her laundry done, and catch up on paperwork. She had lots to do.

Standing at the door with Flora, they were talking about plans for the next day. Flora would go to the market early and buy what she thought was of good value. Flora always said that early morning was the only time to go to the market; otherwise, there would be nothing worthwhile left.

As they were saying good-bye, a car pulled up at the gate, the doors opened, and her colleagues from Namalu got out, collected their bags, and walked into the house. She and Flora moved aside as if to make a guard of honour.

"Hello," was all she could think of saying, and then, "You're welcome."

Nobody replied.

When they'd all gone inside, Flora found her voice and said: "I suppose I'll go back to the kitchen."

Before she could answer, Flora left her standing at the door by herself, and she stood there looking this way and that, as if by looking around she might find an explanation for this sudden visit. No wiser, she shook her head and went inside.

The new arrivals knew the house well and they quickly began establishing themselves in the guest rooms. This was, after all, a guesthouse for all of them working in Karamoja, as well as their regional office and her base.

She went to the kitchen where Flora was already busy assessing what they had and what she could do with it. They were both aware that their guests had been travelling for several hours. They would concentrate on food first and she could seek explanations later.

It didn't take Flora long to decide what to do with what she called her basic ingredients - eggs, onions, tomatoes, cheese, potatoes, chicken, and sausages - that she had lined up in front of her on her workbench. She knew that they all liked sausages, a treat from Nairobi, and she decided to keep these to fry in the morning with the eggs and serve them with the mild German mustard for breakfast. She put these back into the fridge.

Flora chopped some onion, fried it gently in a little oil with fresh garlic and ginger, added some chopped juicy red tomatoes and a little water, pepper, and salt, and left this to cook slowly to make a sauce. She set the potatoes to boil - she knew that these Irish people always liked boiled potatoes - and she smiled as she recalled that these potatoes were known as 'Irish' in the market. In a separate pan, she heated some butter, another treat from Nairobi, and then fried the chicken that she had cut into small pieces. She sprinkled pepper and salt over the chicken, and the aromas wafting out from the kitchen helped everyone to relax.

Soon the guests were setting the table and talking about how hungry they were. Then dinner was served and Flora went home.

Flora's delicious food helped them to relax and they began to tell her why they had come to Mbale.

One colleague, whose job was to coordinate a general food distribution in a number of villages, was told while on her way home for lunch that a rumour had begun circulating that the raiders had decided to kidnap her. This colleague looked like she could be tough, but they knew that she was, at heart, like a coconut.

"This may be a rumour or it may be true," she explained, "but how do I know which?"

By the time their colleague reached home in Namalu, she had decided that she wasn't going to wait there to find out. She asked a driver to drive her to Mbale, and she went in and quickly packed her overnight bag, taking everything she considered important.

As their colleague was leaving the house, other colleagues began to arrive home for lunch.

"Where are you going?" they asked her.

She was reluctant to tell them. She was hoping that she would have left before they returned, and now she felt trapped. They wouldn't let her go without an explanation.

"Wait a minute," one said upon hearing the story. "When and if the raiders come for you, how will they know that you're not here? You can't leave us here; you can't leave here without us."

It was settled then that they would all leave, and within a half-hour they each had a bag packed and were on their way to Mbale.

There was a general understanding that in planning their work they were trying to balance the needs in their programme areas against the risks, and that each person should feel free to leave when they felt that the risks were greater than the needs. The colleague told them that she had decided not to go back to Karamoja; instead, she would stay overnight in Mbale and leave the next morning for Nairobi and then home.

The question now was: what would happen with the programme? No one at the table felt willing or able to take on the newly vacant role.

Before retiring for the night, they reached a compromise. The colleague agreed to travel with her to Kampala the next day to explain the escalating security threats to the UN agencies, WFP and UNICEF, who supplied most of the food for distribution. It would be a one- or two-day trip, and the others would wait in Mbale until they returned. Then the colleague would leave for Nairobi.

They left early the next morning for Kampala. The road was quiet and they made good progress. They met everyone they had hoped to meet, and by early afternoon, it seemed like they might be able to return to Mbale that day. But as they were leaving one office, they were told that the Italian fathers wanted to see them. This was one meeting they hadn't planned for.

As they travelled to the Italian mission, she remembered her first meeting with the Italian fathers in Karamoja about six months earlier. She was travelling with her predecessor, the Big Man, who was handing over responsibilities to her and introducing her to people with whom she would work. At the Italian mission, she was surprised to meet some people who questioned the famine relief work, whereas others were very actively involved and very welcoming. One rather small man was one of the latter. As she was introduced to him, he looked up at the Big Man and then down to her with surprise written all over his face. He looked up and down a couple of times, and then stretched out his hands. As he vigorously shook her hand in both of his, he said: "If he thinks you can do it, you're very welcome indeed."

When they arrived at the Italian mission compound, they were warmly welcomed by a father, who told them that he had both good and bad news for them. He led them into the big dining room, served them coffee and Panettone, and said he would begin with the bad news.

The father told them that their house in Namalu had been attacked by raiders the evening before. As they listened, she watched the colour drain from her colleague's face. The father noticed this too and quickly got to his feet and got some brandy.

After a couple of sips, the colour began to return to her colleague's face. Then she realised that her legs felt like jelly and her hands were shaking. The father, observing all of this, gave her some brandy, too. Then he said that he would like them to listen to the whole story before making any decisions. It went like this:

The two young men who were taking care of the house were there when the raiders arrived. It was just after dark, so they heard them before they saw them. They listened, and when they felt fairly sure about the direction from which the sounds came, they ran to the bathroom to try to escape through the window. The window was very small, and there was time for only one to get out. The other looked for a place to hide and opted to run back to the living room and crawl in under the sofa.

The voices came nearer. There was a crashing noise, the sound of breaking glass, and then the voices were inside the small room and very near the sofa.

It was dark inside too, because the men had extinguished their oil lamps, and so someone was sent outside to collect grass, which was then burned to give light.

The man under the sofa listened to the leader giving instructions. People were sent into the two bedrooms to collect whatever was there, while two others were sent into the kitchen. The plan was that everything would be carried out and piled up underneath a tree, where it would be made ready to be carried away later. While they waited for their instructions to be followed, the leaders sat down on the sofa. They said there was no rush, as there was nobody at home, so they could take all night. They asked for more grass to be brought to burn.

Just as it seemed from his hiding place underneath as if the sofa might soon catch fire from the grass, there were a series of new noises from outside. There was confusion inside, a shot was heard, and the leaders began to panic. They called to everyone inside the house to leave what they were doing and to get out and flee as best they could. There was more shooting and shouting outside, sounds of people running, and then everything went quiet.

The man noticed that flames from the burning grass seemed to be coming closer to the sofa, and then he realised that one of the cushions had caught fire. He decided he must leave his hiding place under the sofa or risk getting burned. As he began to crawl out he heard, with great relief, the voice of his friend who had escaped through the bathroom window.

Together they threw out the burning cushion and thus saved the house from further fire damage. They sat down on the sofa so that his friend could catch his breath and tell his story. This is what he said:

"I ran into the town and straight to the house where I knew people were meeting to organise a local vigilante group. They raised an agreed alarm signal, and soon quite a few people gathered - people who had become members of the group since this type of raiding started a couple of weeks earlier and agreed to come to the rescue if the alarm was raised. I told them what happened and they came straight away with me."

He said that one of the raiders had been shot and one or two others captured, and that people were excited because now they had some clues as to the identity of the raiders.

Outside the house, the rescue team was busy. They decided that the safest thing to do was to carry everything from underneath the tree to the mission, where it could be locked away, and to leave two men to guard the house and what was still in it. They agreed to come back the next morning when it was light to assess the damage to the door and arrange temporary repairs.

Hearing this story at the mission in Kampala she couldn't but remember the mixture of feelings she had during her early days in Uganda. When one Italian sister was shot dead on the road from Moroto, she wanted to leave straight away. But she listened and respected the views of her colleagues who had been longer in the country and who wanted to stay to continue their programme. She empathised with both sides.

But this was the first time she experienced such a strong expression of support by the local community and she felt this outweighed the threats by the raiders, at least for now.

There was some time to go yet before the harvest would be ready, and until then food rations were needed. She felt that she was lucky that she had a choice about leaving or staying, while the local community had none. She knew, though, that the final decision would rest with her colleagues who awaited their return in Mbale: the ones who worked in Karamoja every day.

By the end of the story, it was too late and they were too exhausted to drive back to Mbale. They were invited to spend the night at the mission and to join the fathers for dinner. The latter, especially, was an invitation difficult to resist, because they always served wonderful home-cooked Italian food. She can still remember dribbling olive oil over fresh salad leaves and juicy sliced tomatoes!

She talked on the telephone with her boss, the Big Man, in Dublin, for it had been agreed that all security incidents would be reported immediately. This one, because of the local rescue, presented a new challenge, and her boss agreed that he would come on a field visit as soon as he could arrange flights.

The story of the raid and rescue in Namalu had also reached her colleagues waiting in Mbale, and when she arrived home the next evening, they had already decided what they wanted to do. They wanted to return to Namalu to continue or to complete their work. They suggested that they would stay at the mission and would reassess the situation in a couple of weeks.

They said they were ready to return to Namalu the following day, and she agreed to go with them to discuss new arrangements (necessitated by the departure of one colleague) with the relevant local authorities.

She slept soundly that night and woke early in the morning to pack a new bag. They went to the market in Mbale and stocked up with fresh vegetables and fruit, eggs and coffee. There wasn't much else available, but it was more than could be bought in Karamoja. The coffee was always a great treat from Mbale, as they could go to the local coffee factory and watch as the freshly roasted, locally grown Arabica beans were ground.

They arrived in Namalu in the early afternoon and were warmly welcomed at the mission: the women with the sisters and the men with the fathers. The following day, they were on their way early to their programmes, and she travelled to meet the local authorities in each place. She went to Moroto, Nabilituk, and Amudat, and everywhere she went, they were warmly welcomed back. Everybody seemed happy to see them, to talk about "the great rescue," and the stories grew with each telling.

"We don't want to stay here any longer," was the greeting she heard when she returned to her colleagues at the mission in Namalu after two days.

"We've been to our house," one said, "and the door can easily be repaired. People are working on that. The room is already repainted, the sofa just needs new cushions, and everybody, including the neighbours, agrees that it is safer now than ever before."

What could she say?

Their bags seemed as light as their steps and their mood as they carried them out to their truck. They drove back to their house in the late afternoon sun, and in no time everything was unpacked.

It was late by the time they went to bed that evening. She tossed and turned all night, and was happy when it was morning and time to get up. She left a happy team behind her in Namalu as she set out for Mbale.

* * * * *

Flora had a message for her when she arrived in Mbale in the afternoon. Her boss, the Big Man, would fly into Nairobi the following evening. There was nobody else there in Mbale at that time - nobody else who could go to collect him. She must prepare for another early start and another long eight- or nine-hour journey, this time on her own.

She was grateful for the hot shower and stood under the flowing water for a long time . . . until she couldn't see any more red Karamoja dust in the tray around her feet. Later, she packed her "Nairobi bag," as Flora called it. That was easily done, as Flora had washed and ironed her "Nairobi clothes." She ate a light supper (the delicious chicken and vegetable soup that Flora had prepared), did some accounts, and then went to bed. She was tired, but she slept lightly and was glad when it was time to get up.

It was still dark when the unexpected smell of freshly brewing coffee beckoned from the kitchen. Flora had decided to come in early, as she knew how much the coffee would be appreciated.

As the sun was rising, she reversed out of the garage and was soon on her way. As usual, there wasn't much traffic at this time of the morning, and she made good progress to the border checkpoint.

There was always a long queue of trucks at the border. This was, after all, the then East African Highway that linked landlocked countries like Uganda, Rwanda, Burundi, southern Sudan, and eastern Congo with the port city of Mombasa and the Indian Ocean. (This road is now part of the planned Trans-African Highway that will link the port cities of Mombasa and Lagos.)

She was by now quite familiar with the border-crossing

43

procedures. First, she had to go to the customs office and export the car from Uganda, then to immigration and passport control, then cross no-man's-land, and finally go through the Kenyan immigration and passport control and Kenyan customs to import the car. There were many forms to be filled in and stamped, and entries to be made in big dusty journals. On a good day, the procedures took about one hour. This was a good day for border crossing, as there were not many cars ahead of her. Within fifty-five minutes, she was ready for the final stamp.

The officer in the blue short-sleeved shirt picked up the stamp, hit it against the ink pad - always a welcome sound - and, with the stamp poised in mid-air, said, "I'd like you to give this man a lift."

She was completely taken aback. "I'm sorry," she began, "you know we're not allowed to take strangers in our cars."

"He's not a stranger," the officer in the blue short-sleeved shirt said. "I know him. He has just delivered a car to a mission in Uganda, and he's trying to get home to Nairobi. And I know you," he continued, "because you often pass through here. So, he's not a stranger, and you're not a stranger."

What could she say? Suddenly, all the stories she had heard about hijackings, kidnappings, and car theft flew through her head. At the same time, what he said seemed logical. As she looked at the stamp that hadn't yet hit her passport, she couldn't think of a logical way to refuse this request.

"Okay," she said, "but you will be responsible if anything goes wrong, and these people are my witnesses."

"Okay," the man with the stamp agreed.

In the next instant, she heard the welcome sound of the stamp hitting her passport.

It took about half an hour for her to clear the long line of trucks leaving the border. With their heavy loads, they struggled to build up speed while the fumes from their exhaust pipes were belched out in black clouds.

She felt happy when she cleared all of that and could see

the long road winding its way along the Rift Valley in front of her. There seemed to be new potholes. The new potholes, she had learned, could be more difficult than older ones, as their edges were sharper, not yet smoothed by the traffic.

She hit the first one unexpectedly and hard. After that, on a clearer stretch of road, she felt that the car was a bit more difficult to manoeuvre. The feeling that the back didn't quite follow the front was stronger. The steering pulled to the left in a new way. She stopped, and she and her passenger checked the tyres and the underside of the car. Everything seemed okay. They got back into the car and continued on their long journey.

After a couple of hours, they reached the outskirts of Nakuru. It was hard work, and she was tired. She decided to stop in Nakuru for a cup of tea.

Just as on the journey, her passenger didn't talk much - hardly at all - as they sat at the table in the small café overlooking Lake Victoria and drank their tea. Suddenly, as the waiter came with the bill, she was surprised to hear his voice. "I'd like to drive your car," he said.

Oh, no, she thought as she felt the blood drain out of her face, remembering the warnings.

He noticed her reaction, and before she could say anything, he continued: "This is a long journey. There are still a couple of hours to go before we reach Nairobi ..."

He hesitated while she paid the bill. Then he said, "I can see that you are very tired, and I'd like to help you."

It was true - she did feel very tired. That was the main reason she decided to stop for tea. But she couldn't hand over the keys of the car to a complete stranger. Her organisation had strict rules about who was or could be authorised to drive their vehicles. And insurance was a big issue, as was security. She was responsible for ensuring that the regulations were followed.

It was as if he read her thoughts, for he continued: "Remember, I'm not a stranger. The people at the border know me well."

She thought about her authority to nominate drivers.

Which is worse, she asked herself, *to fall asleep and crash the car, or to lose the car to a thief?*

They decided it was time to leave. As they walked back to the car, she handed him the keys and she got into the passenger seat.

The tea didn't help much, she thought to herself as she felt her heavy eyelids close.

The next thing she remembered was his voice saying: "It's time to wake up; we're almost in Nairobi."

So soon!

"Where do you want to go?" he asked her.

"To Westlands," she replied. "Where do you want to go?"

"I'll go to Westlands," he said.

"But where do you want to go?" she asked, suddenly wide awake. "Where do you live?"

He turned off the main road towards Westlands, pulled the car over to the left of the road, and stopped.

"This will do me," he said as he got out of the car.

He opened the back door to collect his bag, and then held the driver's door open for her.

"But I can't leave you here," she said, confused. "It's like the middle of nowhere."

He handed her the key. "Thank you very much for the lift," he said. "It's been a great help."

Then he turned and walked away, back towards the main road.

Within ten minutes, she was at their Nairobi office and home.

As she sits in her sandy garden in Brantevik looking out as the sun glistens over the Baltic Sea she wonders if all is just a dream?

CHAPTER 6

SIX WEEKS IN EARLY 1993

S till and calm! That's how she remembers the time from when she returned to work in Ireland at the end of 1989 until Somalia began to loom large on her horizon soon after she took up the job of Head of HR in late 1992.

She remembers the very successful recruitment drive for the extensive famine relief programme her organisation launched in Somalia, and the new series of debriefings that she organised for each batch of returnees because high security risks had become part of their day-to-day reality. There were other new things happening too, but none was particularly spectacular. It was busy, but busy was normal.

Then late one morning, she was called to a hastily organised meeting. One of their young Irish volunteers had been shot and seriously wounded in Somalia. That was all they knew. They waited for more information, but none came. The family must be contacted, and that was her job.

On her way back to her desk, she asked a co-worker to come with her but didn't say where to. She simply said that they would leave in five minutes.

They found the house without too much difficulty. They stayed for a while but had no further information before they had to return to their office.

Later that morning a message came in that the young volunteer had died. There were many things to be organised and many things that she, as Head of HR, had to help to coordinate.

She remembers the trip to Frankfurt.

She remembers standing on the tarmac at the American base, watching the plane taxi to a halt, the back come down, and the coffin being wheeled out.

She remembers visiting the undertaker's ancient (it seemed to her) and rambling workshop, where a new coffin had to be organised before they could proceed on their journey to Dublin.

She remembers the helpfulness of the air base staff, the airline staff, and the embassy staff.

She remembers the crowds at the funeral, including the President of Ireland.

She remembers a visit to Somalia a couple of weeks later.

In Somalia, she was reminded of the security meetings in Karamoja. Here again, the big and challenging question was how to balance risks with needs. Nobody else was physically injured in the attack that killed the young volunteer, but the shock and trauma were great, and the security risks were high and growing, as was the famine.

Everyone agreed that, for the time being at least, the needs were greater than the risks and, with renewed efforts for safety, the work would continue.

On the way home from Somalia, she travelled via Nairobi. There she was met with news of another accident. This accident happened a day or two earlier in the northeastern part of Kenya, where a young staff member from one of their border refugee camp programmes had been killed. They asked her to visit the team.

She changed her plans, and a couple of days later, she flew to the recently established tent town at Lokichokio and then continued the journey by road. The young man's brother had been contacted and was on his way north. He arrived the following day.

The brother's only concern was that he could take his brother home and bury him in his village. Her colleagues wanted to comply with the family's wishes as best they could. It took a couple of days of investigating and considering available options. Finally permission was granted to fly the young man's body in one of the small twin-engine private planes (similar to the one she had travelled in to Lokichokio) that were now making regular trips from Nairobi to this relatively isolated place. But there was still one problem.

The plane and the pilot had permission only to fly directly from and to Nairobi. From Nairobi, they promised the brother that they would organise road transport back to his village - only a fraction of the journey from the camps - but the brother was not at all happy with this.

"There is a landing strip near our village," he quietly insisted, "and that is where I want to go."

Their colleagues at their Nairobi office were trying to get permission to land at the airstrip, but it was difficult and slow in coming.

When they began to load the plane for the return journey, they had only been given permission to land at Nairobi. They hadn't given up hope, but it was still unclear what would happen.

The brother sat in the front seat beside the pilot. She sat behind the pilot, beside the young man's body. As the pilot got clearance for take-off, he also got confirmation that he could land at the airstrip on the way. She watched the brother's body visibly relax when he heard this news, despite this being his first flight.

While this was wonderful news for the brother, it presented a situation that was logistically impossible for her and her organisation: there was not enough time for them to help the brother with arrangements from the airfield.

The flight was about two hours, and then in what seemed to her like the middle of nowhere, they began their descent. Soon she could see the airfield: a long straight stretch of laterite in an otherwise undisturbed rural landscape of acacia forest and fields.

Within a couple of minutes they landed, and as they suspected from the air, the place was deserted. They got out of the plane, and together the three of them lifted out the body of the young man. They were quiet as they carried him to the side of the airfield and laid him down on the grass in the limited shade of a small acacia tree.

"This will do fine," the young brother said.

"What will you do now?" she asked him.

"I'll leave my brother resting where he is," he said with great dignity, "while I walk to my village and call people to help me take him home."

"We can't leave you here like this . . ." she began to protest, but the young brother raised both his hands and didn't allow her continue.

"We should be going; my flying time and permissions are limited," the pilot said.

As the young brother thanked them, he shook their hands vigorously with both of his and his eyes brightened, as if reflecting a smile from his soul.

"Thank you so much for leaving me here," he said, "and have a safe flight home."

She watched the young brother walk away from the airfield and out through the bush as the pilot taxied along the airfield, preparing for take-off.

He thanked us as if we had given him a million dollars, rather than leaving him alone with the body of his dead brother, she thought to herself.

* * * * *

About two weeks later, she was trying to finish a project for a course she was undertaking at the IMI in Dublin. She was already late with her submission, but under the circumstances her tutor had granted her an extension.

A telephone call from Tanzania announced that a young volunteer was seriously ill with malaria. He was in a local hospital and she would be updated regularly on his condition.

She made a telephone call to Wales to inform the young volunteer's parents and agreed to keep them updated.

A second call came from Tanzania a couple of hours later

and informed her that the young volunteer was not responding to treatment, that his condition was deteriorating and plans were under way to have him medically flown to Nairobi and, if possibly, home.

The next message came from Nairobi, and the news was bad. Cerebral malaria had been diagnosed, and the young volunteer's condition was considered too ill for him to travel home. Instead, it was suggested that his parents fly to Nairobi to visit him.

The young volunteer's parents had become used to long-distance travel during their working lives but since their retirement they hadn't travelled much. They agreed to fly to Nairobi, and flights were arranged for two days' time, on Sunday.

On Saturday she was at home organising for the next week and working on her project for IMI, as well as keeping in regular contact with her colleagues in Nairobi and updating her colleagues in Dublin. In the afternoon, a message came from Nairobi that the young volunteer's condition had deteriorated further and it was decided that she should travel to Nairobi with the young volunteer's parents the next day.

She flew from Dublin to Heathrow on Sunday morning and met the parents. They had travelled by train from North Wales and arrived at Heathrow a short time before her. They checked in together for their flight to Nairobi and proceeded to the transit lounge. There, in the middle of the busy transit area of Terminal 3, she got a message that the young volunteer had died.

She remembers a woman in a British Airways uniform who was especially kind and helpful, and took care of the young volunteer's parents while she answered telephone calls.

After an initial hesitation, it was agreed that the three of them would continue their journey to Nairobi, and their seats were calmly and efficiency upgraded to business class. They were shown into a small room where they were grateful for the privacy it afforded them. She was given access to a telephone, and within a very short time she had made all the necessary arrangements for local undertakers to facilitate the return of the young volunteer's body.

She remembers being met on arrival at the airport the next morning by all their team members in Nairobi and sitting in the little café waiting for her luggage (which didn't arrive), while her colleagues carefully explained to the parents all that they knew about the short history of their son's illness.

She remembers borrowing a change of clothing from one Nairobi colleague and going to the funeral home, while she sent her own clothes to the laundry.

She remembers accompanying the young volunteer's parents to the funeral home and her own sense of shock after learning that the young volunteer, her son, was the first dead body the mother had seen.

She remembers the funeral service organised for the late afternoon and nothing more until they returned to the airport the next morning with all arrangements made for the coffin to travel on the same flight back to London.

As they checked in for their flight, she was given her luggage, which had arrived with that incoming flight, and it was duly checked in for the return.

She remembers arriving in Heathrow and going to a cargo terminal where the young volunteer's mother was given an opportunity to meet with her son on his final homeward trip— she remembers watching the mother looking at the crate in the undertaker's van that carried her son's coffin, and then watching as the van was driven away to Wales.

She remembers the wipers on the windscreen during the long drive in the rain from Heathrow back to the young volunteer's home in north Wales.

She remembers little of the ferry journey back to Dublin the following day.

She remembers her neighbour asking her when she arrived home on Wednesday morning if she had been away somewhere nice for the weekend.

She remembers being surprised that the flowers in her living room that she bought on Saturday morning were still fresh.

Back in her office in Dublin, she had a call from her tutor. Certificates for the course were being presented the following week on Friday evening and he wanted her to know that she was very welcome to attend. If she still wanted to finish her project, he told her, she must submit it by Wednesday evening. If she did, he would read it on Thursday and the external examiner from Trinity College (TCD) had agreed to read it on Friday. If it were good enough, she would get a certificate.

As she was presented with her Certificate in Human Resource Management that Friday evening, the external examiner congratulated her, saying it was one of the best projects he had read.

She remembers that for a long time after those six weeks, tears rolled down her cheeks every time she drove alone in her car.

CHAPTER 7

A TRIP TO THE LAKE

The rattling of the rain on the tin roof woke all three of them shortly after 3:00 a.m. It wasn't unusual to have rain at this time of the year, but they were hoping it wouldn't rain that day.

This is not what we need today she thought to herself as she put the alarm clock back on the shelf and turned over to try to get more sleep. But it was impossible. After a while, she settled into the rhythm of the rain, and as she listened, she found herself reflecting on how comfortable the room was, considering it was a converted old container.

The walls were plastered and painted cream and the curtains and bedcover had a cream background with small blue flowers. The bed was comfortable too, even if a little narrow, and there was a nice handmade rug on the floor beside the bed.

The rain became heavier and made a terrible racket. She knew that if it didn't stop soon, their journey that day would be more difficult. She hoped it might only be a local downpour that wouldn't last long or wouldn't affect the roads.

She remembered when her friend insisted that she had to make this journey and that she had to make it soon. Her friend then agreed to travel with her and they agreed on this date.

She travelled from Kampala (a journey of about four hours) the day before in lovely sunshine. She arrived in the late afternoon. Over a tasty dinner of chicken and rice, a colleague of her friend announced that she would join them on the trip, so they would be three.

Before going to bed, they checked their jeep and packed a shovel, a rope, and drinking water - the local staples for travelling in that area - as well as supplies for the friend they hoped to meet at the lake.

By 6:oo a.m., they had showered, dressed, finished their breakfast of coffee, toast, and boiled eggs, and were ready to leave. It was beginning to get bright, but it was still raining. Travelling in the dark, they knew, was risky, because the gravel roads were narrow and not signposted. There wasn't much traffic, but many of the small trucks that travelled the route had no lights or reflectors. The road wound its way through small villages and cultivated fields of matoke (savoury banana), and was criss-crossed by grazing animals that were used to wandering as they pleased.

Travelling in the rain was risky too, because with the water the surface of the road in some places turned into thick slippery mud. As they travelled out of the town, left the tarred road, and turned on to the gravel road, the rain seemed to get heavier.

Ordinarily, they would not go to the lake during the week or if there was any hint of rain. But this was special, and in a strange way, the rain seemed appropriate - as if the heavens could no longer hold their grief but poured it out in big fat raindrops. These big fat raindrops now collected into little streams that made their way along the road, and as they did so, the gravel seemed to become less and less, the mud more and more.

It was bright now, but it was a grey day and their progress was slow. More people were moving about - women with water containers on their heads, children in blue and white uniforms on their way to school, small boys with animals - and they had to be very careful. They were aware that having to apply the brakes in this situation could be very risky.

They travelled on.

There were fewer villages now, fewer cultivated fields. The grey clouds were lower and the rain had changed; now it was finer, the air was cooler, and everything seemed soaked. There wasn't much chat between them.

Around midday, as they turned a bend in the road, they saw their friend who sat at her desk in the makeshift office that she had arranged in front of her tent. Her office consisted of a picnic table with attached benches and a large sun umbrella that now sheltered her from the rain. Fortunately, there was no wind and the fine rain fell straight down. It ran off the umbrella in big drops and fell into the channels she had dug around her table and tent. She had succeeded, for now at least, in keeping her space dry.

Their friend served them coffee in plastic mugs from a large blue thermos flask, and for a few seconds, they were lost in its wonderful aroma. As they drank the hot coffee, their friend told them a little about her work and gave them directions to the lake. She told them that it was easy to find from here - they just had to follow the tracks of the trucks.

Revived by meeting their friend and sharing her coffee, they set out for the lake. The road, as they continued, was like a mud bath, and they were quite impressed with the performance of their 4wd car and with the fact that they still moved forward. Soon enough they could see the lake in front of them and three or four working trucks.

She thought the fine rain seemed to be a little lighter here as they got out and started to follow the men working with the trucks. But they had to hold on to each other as their feet slipped and slid in the mud. Soon enough, they reached the sandy beach and the lake spread out in front of them.

Even on this grey day, the lake was a wonderful sight. She reflected briefly on its vastness. Lake Victoria is one of the largest lakes in the world and is almost the same size as Ireland!

They walked a little farther and then stopped to watch the men at work. It could have been a fishing scene: men were dressed in waterproofs, some green and some yellow, and waded into the water with their nets. Others, farther out, hauled their nets in and emptied them into their boats, while others brought the nets and boats ashore and loaded the trucks.

She watched all this happen with a quiet steady rhythm that seemed to match the wind, the waves, and the rain.

When one truck was full and started to move away, they were beckoned to follow and they walked and slid back to their car.

They followed the truck for a mile or so back along the muddy road they had come on and then veered off to the left. Here the road was a little better: more gravel and less mud. The rain was still light.

They followed the truck along the road as it wound its way around the edge of a quarry. Near its end the road widened out, and here there were more trucks and some diggers at work: digging, unloading, and filling in.

They parked their car a little distance from the trucks and diggers, and walked to the edge of the quarry to watch. A few vultures flew overhead, and their mournful cries were almost, but not quite, drowned out by the sounds of the trucks and diggers.

She noticed a couple of the huge and unmistakable Marabou Storks. She didn't like Marabou Storks. With their massive grey bills, naked pinkish heads with a white ruff at the base, and bare pendent throat pouches, she thought they were ugly. But with so many of them living around Kampala, she was beginning to feel like the gardener who had tried everything, unsuccessfully, to rid himself of the unwanted dandelions in his lawn - she was learning to love them. And it was easy for her to admit that the Marabou Storks were wonderful gliders.

The truck they followed from the lake drove along the newly made road to where the other trucks and diggers worked and reversed to the edge of the quarry, where its back began to tip up. They waited and watched, but nothing else seemed to happen. Then they gasped as the load suddenly fell into the quarry.

As the truck moved away, a digger moved into place and tipped in its load of white powder - lime. The truck drove away and headed back to the lake to collect another load.

They stood for a long time, as if glued to the spot. They were the only three silent witnesses to the burial of people - men, women, and children - they didn't know.

Many refused to believe the stories that had begun circulating a couple of weeks earlier of brutal killings in Rwanda and bodies thrown into the river until the bodies started arriving into Lake Victoria in Uganda. Now there were thousands: bodies that had travelled from Rwanda, through Tanzania, and into the lake in Uganda. Nobody in Uganda knew who any of them were, by name, by family or by village.

She remembered, with almost disbelief, the stories she heard from Rwanda: stories of hate that were broadcast over a radio station and warned people to kill or be killed, followed by the mass murder of neighbour by neighbour, family member by family member - "genocide" some called it.

She watched the Marabou Storks gliding above the pit and

recalled Jack Boyle in Seán O'Casey's *Juno and the Paycock* quoting the Scottish poet Robert Burns (1759–1796): "Man's inhumanity to man makes countless thousands mourn."

Their silent tears were washed away by the rain.

CHAPTER 8

BE ON TIME!

"Stop!"

Her heart missed a beat. She held her breath, steadied her grip on the steering wheel, and carefully applied the brakes. But the back of the car slid towards the left bank of the road.

"Stop!" This time it sounded different.

"I can't," she said. "The car is sliding in the mud."

"Stop!"

"Stop what?" she asked, beginning to panic. "I'm not doing anything."

She turned her head and looked over her left shoulder at the one who sat in the back seat, and to her horror she saw that his head was out through the rear passenger window which was closing on his neck.

She saw him turn his body to ease the pressure and discomfort. As he turned, she saw his knee move away from the electric window control and the pressure ease. She understood what to do, and quickly turned around and found the window controls on the driver's door. She opened the window and he flopped back into his seat. The crisis was over.

"Oh, my god!" she heard herself say as she looked over her shoulder again and watched the contortions vanish from his face.

"Oh, my god!" she said again. "How could that happen? Are you all right?"

It was early on Sunday morning. They had not planned this trip to the hospital. He had a tight travel schedule and had been warned that he must be on time because the car would leave at 2:00 p.m. and could not wait. He knew that this was not an idle threat, that travel regulations were serious and unlike the East African flexible approach to time.

This unplanned trip to the hospital was all because of the colour of the paint.

She was the one locally responsible for administering her organisation's support to the hospital rehabilitation, as well as the road rehabilitation projects, because both the regional hospital and the regional roads network were the responsibility of the central ministries rather than of the district administration. At the same time, they were high priority projects for people in the district.

The two projects were progressing reasonably well, and the mood in the district had been very positive since her organisation had agreed to fund them. They were not, after all, high priorities for her organisation, nor were they much appreciated - they were more tolerated like a stone in one's shoe. They were often affectionately referred to as "the bloody road" or "the bloody hospital."

She sometimes felt like "the meat in the sandwich," being pressed by both sides, but she was mostly happy enough to play this role as it facilitated the "real" work that her organisation wanted to support in the district: primary schools, water and sanitation, and primary health care.

The programme was designed with a participatory approach and a strong focus on partnership, and it had been agreed that the ultimate decision maker was the local district administration, her organisation's main partner. She liked this, and it was one of the things that made her work interesting and satisfying. But sometimes it could be very challenging.

Now it is paint, she thought. In the overall scheme of

things, she wondered how it could be so that paint was the topic on everybody's lips this weekend. She didn't really have time to talk about paint. Her visitor was beginning a new assignment, and she had just agreed to go to Goma in Eastern Zaire (now Congo) within the next few days.

Paint! It couldn't possibly be that important. Wouldn't any paint be better than it was? She mused.

Her initial reaction was to dismiss this issue. But no, this was not how people felt about it. Everyone she met, it seemed, wanted to tell her how awful this new paint colour was. When people sensed that she was beginning to listen to what they wanted to say about paint colour, they told her how good the new road was. They assured her that it wouldn't take more than an hour to drive from Kibaale to the hospital in Kagadi, and there she could see for herself.

By Saturday evening, she had been convinced that they could leave Kibaale at 6:00 a.m. and be back there by 9:00 a.m., have a second breakfast, and then leave for Kampala, which they said she could reach by 1:30 p.m. at the latest.

"There is plenty of time for your visitor to be in time for his 2:00 p.m. departure," they told her.

* * * * *

On that Sunday morning, they woke up to the smell of freshly brewed coffee and the sounds of birdsong. The shower water was still warm from the solar heating the day before. As they sat at the table in the central courtyard to drink their coffee and eat the freshly made toast with butter, the sky began to lighten in the east, heralding a beautiful day.

They could see that the work on the road was progressing well as they made good progress on the new gravel surface of the widened road. Then they came to a section that had been widened and the new under-layers were being compacted. It was wet and they assumed this to be part of the roadworks.

Soon the sky began to darken as very heavy clouds moved in, and then they met the rain.

No, no, no! Not here! Not here and not now! she thought desperately.

This part of the road seemed to be just mud, and soon enough they were sliding and slipping, even with 4wd and a good solid car. At times they slipped along sideways and forwards, while at other times the wheels turned but they didn't move at all.

He colleague and driver, decided he would get out with the shovel and try to find gravel or other material to put under the wheels for grip. He asked her to get into the driver's seat and follow his instructions from outside, while he asked their visitor to sit in the back for the time being and report on what was happening on that side of the road. He suggested that they rotate these tasks for as long as necessary to keep them moving.

Somebody else - a road worker or a pedestrian, she didn't know which - helped by throwing branches and leaves in front of the tyres to create some grip. It was slow work, but they were making progress and moving in the right direction.

That was when their visitor was almost strangled in the window.

Two hours later, when they arrived at the hospital in bright sunshine, they were not in much of a good mood to discuss paint colour. Rather, it had become an irritation. But paint colour was what everybody they met enthusiastically wanted to talk about.

They walked around the hospital, beginning at the rebuilt

outpatient department with its waiting areas arranged around the central square minor theatre and treatment rooms. There were individual consulting and minor treatment rooms along each of the four outside walls. The smell of new paint was fresh.

Okay, she thought, *not my choice of colours, but so what?*

She can't remember what colour the walls were, but all the window frames - and they were many, all the way around the central square and along the outside walls - were orange. They were mostly silent as they were led through the different buildings, with the orange paint used in different combinations throughout.

As they went into the fourth block, where the orange had been painted onto the walls, their visitor very quietly said, "Jesus Christ, it's awful."

By the end of their tour, they found it hard to disagree with the general opinion that even healthy people came away from these new colours in the hospital feeling ill.

Could colour really be so powerful? she wondered.

In her ignorance about colour schemes, she thought the orange on the window frames seemed okay, but on the walls it was disastrous.

She talked with the painter who was working away in a new block and asked him to stop using the orange paint. He was doubtful; he said he was following clear instructions and he had a tight deadline to meet.

They slipped and slid on their return journey back to Kibaale as the rain belt seemed to travel just in front of them. Finally, they were back on the gravel road and, almost magically, out of the rain belt.

They knew they were late on their return to Kampala, but they tried not to think about it.

Maybe we will have some luck, she hoped.

About a half-hour before their destination in Kampala, they noticed one of their visitor's new colleagues standing outside a filling station. They stopped.

"We couldn't wait for you" the new colleague told them, "but now there is some problem with our car, and it's being fixed. You might be lucky . . . if you rush back to collect your things."

Not many words were exchanged as their visitor collected his bag and equipment a little while later. He knew he had been warned to be on time.

CHAPTER 9

THE MAN WITH THE PEN

This was the kind of telephone call she hated. He was a nice man, this one who called her from Dublin, but she hated to hear his voice on the telephone. He didn't call often, but when he did, it was with a difficult request.

"The President wants to visit Goma again," he told her, "and we want you to go there next week to coordinate the preparations for her visit."

What could she do?

There were problems with the painting at Kagadi hospital, and she had a lot of work to do in Kampala.

She was now her organisation's "expert" on Goma (in what was then Eastern Zaire, now Congo). She had been there twice before, and this would be her second time to co-ordinate local arrangements for the President's visits.

She remembered when she took this job in 1994 how happy she felt when a friend told her that she wouldn't have to worry about emergencies for a couple of years. "There won't be any emergency relief work in your new assignment in Uganda," he had said.

That seemed a long time ago now.

She liked President Mary Robinson. She was very impressed with the way the President saw people, not as groups or crowds, but as individuals - how she empathised with the plight of refugees as people who had lived through some terrible experiences, including genocide, murder, forced movement from their homes and families, and then mass deaths from hunger, cholera, and other diseases (diseases that thrived in overcrowded conditions with insufficient food and with major water and sanitation problems).

She remembered her first visit to Goma in 1994 and the fine black volcanic ash that hung in the air like fog and covered all surfaces. She remembered how the trees seemed to vanish at lightning speed, how the tree-lined avenues of the mornings were shadowless with exposed stumps in the afternoons; how the bodies piled up in the central islands of the roads because graves could not be dug fast enough in the volcanic rock to bury them; how the cholera patients lay packed like sardines in a tin in the hospital tents and her thoughts that those with someone to hold up their drips were the lucky ones!

She remembered thinking that of all the places she had worked and all the scenes she had witnessed over twenty years, this was the closest representation of hell she had yet experienced.

She remembered walking with the President through one of the hospital tents in Goma the year before, when one of the President's aides signalled to the President that it was time to leave. She was very impressed with how the President quietly and with no fuss acknowledged the message but said she had to greet the other patients, too. As they walked up and down the lines of beds, the President warmly greeted each patient. As they left the hospital, the President quietly said to her: "These people have waited so patiently."

Yes, she thought, *I am proud of my President and her way with people.*

She had no option, in a way, but she was also happy to agree to this assignment, and soon she was finalising her travel plans and then it was time to go.

The Head of Protocol would meet her in Nairobi the next day. They would travel to Kigali, Rwanda, together, and then she would continue on to Goma. The plan was that the President would visit Rwanda one day and Goma the next. The Head of Protocol would coordinate arrangements in Kigali, and she would coordinate arrangements in Goma. At the end of the visit, they would travel back to Kampala with the President's party.

A couple of days later she was in Goma.

The killer threat this time was not cholera or disease but security. In the past month or so, land mines had become the thing that people feared most, as there had been many accidents. Now mine sweepers - trucks with special mine detection equipment - had to check the roads every morning before the UN gave clearance for aid workers to travel to their workplaces in the refugee camps.

This new security protocol added to the general air of tension between those charged with security of their personnel and those who just wanted to get on with their work. Some of the latter found the precautions tedious, even though a number of their colleagues or co-workers had been injured when their vehicles drove over land mines on the roads.

Another cause of tension was a growing feeling that this emergency aid programme had passed its "best before date." There were allegations that aid workers were helping those who were responsible for the genocide the year before. That was said to be the reason they were too afraid to go home as other refugees had done.

These tensions reminded her of the fear that was almost palpable one year earlier.

She noticed with sympathy that local leaders of aid groups seemed numbed by the complex situation in which they found themselves. They too questioned their role, but because the refugee numbers were still high, they felt unwilling or unable to recommend a withdrawal - unable to decide.

She felt she was lucky. In the midst of this confusion, her role was simply to organise for a smooth and safe visit for the President.

Very soon she had many people working enthusiastically with her. They seemed happy to have a break from the constant questioning of their roles and to have a definite task, even for a week. They all liked the President, too.

At one level, these preparations reminded her of her days as a teenager in the local drama group in her home village of Rathcoole in Co. Dublin. Often it was like building a new set.

"Can you change that wall? Can you make a door there, a window here, a pathway along here, an entrance on this side, and an exit over there?" she asked as she visited the different programmes. It was a hive of activity.

"Will this visit really happen?" they asked her as she returned from daily security meetings with news of more land-mine accidents.

"I don't know," was all she could answer. "But I'm told that we have to act as if it will until we know definitely that it won't."

After yet another accident along the road, she had to stop as she was giving the standard reply. She looked down and noticed the goosebumps and hairs standing on her arms. Her new friend, head of one of the NGOs, looked down and noticed this, too. They looked at each other with tears in their eyes, and then her new friend said, "It's okay; I understand."

That was the last time anyone asked her if the visit would go ahead.

The weather was lovely. There was no rain, it was not too hot, there was plenty of shade from the sun, and the forecast was good. It should be perfect weather for the visit.

Now it was the day before the visit. Everything was ready and spirits were high. But there was one remaining problem: they still didn't have permission for the President's plane to land. Most of the arrangements had been made, but one paper still had to be signed and the man with the pen - as the one who was authorised to sign was called - was away.

Suddenly, someone rushed into the room where she was having a light lunch of soup and bread and said: "The man with the pen is back and you must go and see him now."

She didn't recognise the roads the driver took, but he didn't speak much English and she didn't speak any French, so their conversation was very limited. Finally he stopped at big gates that seemed to be well guarded. He spoke with one of the guards, who sent a team to check their car. Then he gave a signal, the gates opened, and they drove in.

Their car stopped in front of the steps that led up to two big brown wooden doors and he simply said, "Go in."

She was hesitant as she approached the doors and knocked, but nobody answered.

He called to her. "Go in," he said again.

She saw that one of the big brown doors was open. It made a small creaking sound as she pushed it in. She waited a moment, and then walked into a dark hallway. She listened for sounds and then walked towards voices she heard in a room to the right-hand side of the hall.

It was a large room, furnished with heavy dark wood furniture, a couple of large sofas, and armchairs. There were two men standing near the centre of the room talking on telephones. Over in the corner to the far right, a group of five or six men sat in sofas around a large coffee table. Some of them stood up as she entered.

"Come and join us," one said.

Another added, "Have some whiskey."

They made space and invited her to sit in an armchair.

"I'm sorry for disturbing you and for coming without an appointment . . ." she began.

"Sit down, sit down - join us and have some whiskey," a couple of them said at the same time. She was ushered towards the armchair.

"Which whiskey would you like?" one asked, and then added "You can see that we have many."

She remembered her good friend with whom she had learned to appreciate good whiskey many years ago, and she smiled to herself as she spotted the bottle of Jameson Gold Reserve, one of his favourites. She thought about how much he would appreciate this scene.

Do I have time to drink whiskey now? she wondered to herself. She knew she didn't, but on the other hand, could she refuse? She thought she couldn't even though the woman sitting opposite said she was drinking water.

She chose a Jameson.

They were impressed as she joked that it was because she was representing her country, Ireland.

As she watched the golden liquid being poured over the ice into a beautiful crystal glass, she thought, *what a good Jameson advertisement this would make!*

They saluted and clinked glasses.

She started to explain why she was there. She said she had been told that the plane carrying her President the next day would only be allowed to land if the paper she had in her hand was signed.

She held out her papers as she spoke, and one man asked to see her letter of introduction. It was written on embassy paper from Uganda, signed by the Head of Protocol, and it thanked everyone in advance for assistance given to her in her work representing her country. Her papers were passed around for inspection.

"Your President has been here before?" someone said.

"Yes, she was here last year," another answered.

"This is the paper that I'm told has to be signed before the President's plane can land tomorrow," she said, holding out the paper.

"Can I see it?" one of them asked, and she handed it across the table to him.

He read it slowly, showed it to the men on either side of him, and then passed it to the woman sitting opposite her. She watched in amazement as the woman took a pen from her bag and signed the paper.

The woman handed the paper back to a man who handed it back to her. He then lifted his glass, and said: "Sláinte; is that the right way to say it?"

She smiled, lifted her glass, and said: "Sláinte"!

The next morning, as they stood in line in the sunshine waiting for the President's flight to land, she recognised some faces and smiled as a few men winked at her.

Much later, back in Kampala, with the visit successfully over, she reflected on the changes she had observed in just a year.

For the first time she had seen the beauty of Lake Kivu. She understood that she had lived within one kilometre of the lake during her first stay in 1994, but because of the black volcanic ash and fog that hung in the air and covered every surface, she never saw the lake. The other remarkable thing to her was how the trees along the wide avenues had re-grown and how the flowers in the central islands created a great splash of colour.

CHAPTER 10

NOW WHAT WOULD YOU LIKE TO TALK ABOUT?

"It is worse," the young boy said. "Worse?" she asked. "That's what everybody's saying," the young boy answered.

The young boy - ten years old - had come to greet her at the guesthouse. He had lived in the district with his parents for two years now. He was an inquisitive child, the only white child who lived and attended school in the district - his older siblings were at school in Ireland - and he knew everything that was going on. He loved to talk with people, and he wasn't shy. He noticed every new visitor, and before they had their bags unpacked, he knew what their business in the district was about.

"How could it be worse?" she wondered out loud.

"They say that even if you go in well, you come out sick," the young boy continued.

Then he remembered why he was there. "Have you anything you'd like to put in our fridge?" he asked her.

This had become the routine since they had the new gas fridge at his house. She still had to bring all her own supplies when she came to stay in the district because there were no shops or markets yet in that place.

As soon as she arrived at the guesthouse, or as soon as he came from school, he came and collected what was best kept cool and took it home to their fridge. Then in the mornings before going to school, he came to the guesthouse with cold milk and cheese for her breakfast.

She had just returned from Goma, and it didn't take long

for her to realise that what the young boy said was true. Everybody wanted to talk to her about paint and everybody said the colour was worse.

That is, until she thought she might be able to help change it. When she asked, most people commented that there were too many "important things" that needed attention and that the painting was almost finished.

"Finished?" she asked, disappointed but not really surprised. She remembered when she had asked the painter to stop that he had said he had a tight deadline to meet.

"Yes," she was told, "it's almost finished."

Okay, that's the end of that, then, she thought.

Paint is not my priority, she thought to herself.

And she remembered that paint certainly was not the priority of her organisation. Even hospital rehabilitation was not their priority. They were interested in supporting basic education, primary health care, water, and sanitation. They wanted to talk about the number of children attending school, both boys and girls, the number of new classrooms built, the number of functioning wells, the number of latrines in use, the number of children vaccinated, and so on and so forth.

These were her priorities, too. But she understood that the hospital and roads were top priorities for the District and she had inherited her organisation's commitment to support the rehabilitation of the district hospital and the reconstruction of the roads, and she had responsibility for administering these projects.

When she talked about schools, classrooms, vaccinations, water, latrines, and so on, people in the District listened politely, and when she was finished, they said: "What about the paint?"

"Well, what about the paint?" she replied.

"It is making people sick," they told her. "It has to be changed."

"What do you know about paint and colour schemes?" people asked her when she brought up the topic.

She remembered how they had experimented with paint as she grew up and were allowed to help their dad with painting their childhood home. She remembered their experiment with colours in her sister's new home; she could still see the stripes of colour painted on the wall of the hall directly opposite the front door that stayed there for years.

"I know nothing about colour," she answered, "but I know that something is wrong with the new colour scheme at Kagadi Hospital because so many people are upset about it."

"It is time that people got used to new colour schemes in hospitals," some suggested. "Hospitals need to be brightened up."

She heard about other district hospitals where people were very happy with new colour schemes and she hoped that the people in Kagadi would be happy too when they got used to the change.

But time showed itself not to be a healer in this situation. People did not grow to like these new colours; they wanted them changed.

She remembered and was happy that when her organisation's development cooperation work in Kibaale District in western Uganda was begun a participatory approach had been agreed on, with the district acting as the primary decision maker. The district hospital was under the responsibility of the Ministry of Health and not the district administration, but it had become the primary interest of everybody in the district. The paint issue was now affecting other relationships. The district administration didn't have the authority to change the colours and they wanted her to do it.

She remembers the feeling that it was a "filling in the sandwich" situation, as an old friend used to say. She felt she was being pressed in from both sides. She also felt that paint was a relatively minor issue, or that it should be. But it was becoming too much of a distraction, and she wanted to stop that.

Her instinct told her that it was important to pay attention to what people were saying. The "sandwich" feeling was the struggle going on between her head (logic) and her heart (intuition). She remembered a rather heated discussion many years earlier, where some insisted that men were logical and women were intuitive.

If only it were that simple.

She was a "fixer" - she had always been a "fixer." She hated bullying, and she was not good at confrontation. She easily overlooked difficult situations if they only concerned herself. But she felt obliged to act against unfairness or disadvantage that impacted others, especially others with no voice, or whose voice wouldn't be heard. That was just how she was.

As a fixer, she had no choice; she must act.

A friend agreed to join her on a picnic to Mount Elgon at the weekend. She hadn't been in the northeast of Uganda since she worked in Karamoja in 1981–82, and now it was the mid 1990s.

She remembered when she had been introduced to the mountain and how much they used to enjoyed those occasional Sunday afternoon picnics and the panoramic views from the plateau at the top. Now she had an opportunity to revisit the mountain because one of the hospitals that was said to be happy with a new colour scheme was in Mbale, the town at the foot of the mountain, where she had lived.

They left Kampala early on the Sunday morning. Their plan was to visit the hospital first and then go up the mountain for the picnic, for which she had found a Panettone (the Italian Christmas cake with the wonderful distinctive aroma).

The trip to the mountain was not such a happy one that day. As they travelled from the hospital, they could see a mist rolling over the top of the mountain. The mountain road was narrow, and they met rain about halfway up. The mountainside was much more densely populated and more extensively cultivated than she remembered. As they went higher, they saw that parts of the road had been washed away.

As the rain changed into mist, they understood that they wouldn't be able to make it to the top of the mountain for a picnic that day. But the road was narrow and they had to travel on and up in the mist for quite a while before they found a place wide enough for them to turn around.

Travelling down, they were finally happy to be out of the mist and then out of the rain. They found a place on the dry plains with no view where they at least enjoyed their picnic. The Panettone, though, was as good as she remembered it!

While their picnic was disappointing, their visit to the hospital was enlightening. Very quickly they understood why people were happy with the new colour scheme there. It was bright and fresh with pale off-white walls enlivened by dark blue, yellow, and red painted on door frames, door handles, railings, and small pillars.

She now felt confident that she could support the people in Kagadi when they said that they would never get used to their new colour scheme with orange painted on large walls. She understood that both the colour, and the use of colour, was inappropriate.

* * * * *

Soon after their "Mount Elgon outing," as she referred to it, she met, by chance, the manager of the paint factory in Kampala. When they were introduced, the woman told her that she had heard about problems with paint at the hospital in Kagadi and added that she wasn't surprised.

"I've worked with paint for many years and haven't had an order like this before," the woman said.

WOW! This is like opening a door and letting fresh air in, she thought.

The woman even told her that she knew which one was the offending colour. The woman offered to blend it with white in two or three different proportions, paint them on a wall at the factory, and have her come and choose the best one.

She wasn't prepared to make any decisions about paint or colour by herself, so she contacted the people at the hospital. They enthusiastically agreed that they wanted to take up the paint manager's offer and wanted to participate in the colour selection. A date was agreed when they would come to Kampala and go together to the paint factory and decide.

She was ready, as agreed, at 9:00 a.m. on the appointed morning. They didn't have much time - only an hour - because the paint factory manager had another appointment. So far they were three: the hospital medical superintendent, the district engineer, and herself. She was anxious to go, but the other two asked her to wait because there were more people, members of the hospital management committee, on the way.

The time ticked away, and they drank coffee and chatted about this and that. The paint factory manager telephoned to find out where they were. She told them that everything was ready and waiting for them, and reminded them of her next

78

appointment. But the other people from the hospital still hadn't arrived. This was before the mobile phone era, and they had no way of knowing where they were.

With about fifteen minutes left before the paint factory manager's next appointment, they decided they must go. A colleague at the office agreed that when and if the other people arrived, she would bring them to the paint factory.

At the paint factory, they quickly and easily agreed that they didn't like any of the shades of orange painted on the big wall. The paint factory manager agreed with them. She showed them into a small room with a table and a couple of chairs, gave them some colour charts, told them they were welcome to stay as long as they liked, and wished them good luck as she bade them farewell and left for her next meeting.

Looking at the colour charts in that little grey room with its small window, she wondered how one could choose from those hundreds of 5 cm square blobs.

I have no idea; it's like looking into a bush, she thought.

Just as they were about to give up - each one admitting that they knew nothing about paint - there was a commotion at the door and two man rushed in. They were out of breath and scolded them for not waiting for him.

"How are we expected to find our way around this city?" they seemed to say together and continued: "Is there no humanity left in this world? When did time become so important?"

All this seemed to come out in one breath before one flopped down into the chair that someone had moved over towards him.

"That's it," he said, pointing his finger to a pale green patch on the chart.

"No, there is no need for any other colour change," he said

in response to their surprised questions. "The orange can stay on the window frames and on some doors. It is just the orange walls that have to be repainted."

And it was as simple as that.

* * * * *

On her next visit to the district, everybody talked about paint.

Not again! she thought.

This time, though, people wanted to compliment her on the wonderful healthy change at the hospital. Even people who said they were colour-blind claimed that they had been able to see the offending orange colour.

"It's good that we sent an artist to select the colour," they proudly told her.

"Now what would you like to talk about?" the district officials asked her.

She smiled and said, "The Pachwa Road."

"Ah!" they said as she watched the smiles grow and broaden on their faces, too.

"The Pachwa Road"!

She remembers how the Pachwa Road had been everybody's favourite topic before paint took over for a while. But now everything was back to normal, she thought.

The Pachwa Road ran almost directly north from the new district headquarters in the centre of Kibaale District, to Hoima, the neighbouring district. It was part of the district's internal network of feeder roads (rural district roads).

She remembers the early study that concluded that none of Kibaale's estimated 600 kilometres of feeder roads was in a maintainable condition - that all needed to be rehabilitated. This had presented a real challenge to her and her colleagues.

Roads were not listed as a priority for her organisation. She remembered her research for her Masters Degree and how issues with roads could be theoretical and academic. For example, if roads were considered a public good in economic terms, then it could be argued that all would benefit from having better roads, having better access, having easier travel. Otherwise when the costs and benefits of roads were analysed, it was more difficult to prioritise road rehabilitation in a poverty-oriented programme because most benefit went to those who had more to be transported along the roads to markets. Economic justification required complex estimations of the value of better roads, the distribution of that value between different income or wealth groups, and the possible negative consequences to the environment and society.

She was familiar with these issues; she had written about them a number of years earlier.

In Kibaale District in the early 1990s, there were other considerations, too. When the roads were impassable, it was difficult to argue that anybody benefited, while other works like school building or school rehabilitation were more difficult and more expensive because of the difficulties of access. It was for these reasons that her organisation reluctantly agreed to support road rehabilitation as well as the hospital rehabilitation projects. They were thought of as essential components of creating an enabling environment for poverty work.

She remembers how the question of how Kibaale's feeder roads should be rehabilitated had challenged all of them, for months. She remembered the early study that recommended using labour-based methods. This, the argument went, was to ensure that benefits from the work itself, as well as the longer-term benefits of better roads, would be distributed to local communities and to women.

The biggest problem or challenge with this recommendation was the lack of experience of labour-based road rehabilitation, not only in the district, but also in the country. For this reason, the study recommended beginning with an easy stretch of road close to the district headquarters during which skills could be developed.

"Time wasting" was what most people in the district thought of this suggestion. "Let's do the road that will be most beneficial," they argued, "and that is the Pachwa Road."

People remembered the bus service that operated along the Pachwa Road to Hoima up to about twenty-five years earlier. "So we know it's possible," they argued.

She remembered that this was the stage at which she came into the picture.

In their first meeting, the consultant told her about all of these issues and that the Pachwa Road was, most likely, the most difficult stretch of road in the whole district because there were two or three swamps to be crossed. It was all overgrown, so it was impossible to assess.

"We need heavy machines to do this work, and we need a surveyor and contractor who can organise and do it" had become the general argument.

She remembers the number of attempts that had been made to assess the work to be done on the Pachwa Road. After each attempt, the assessment teams walked back to the district headquarters - usually splashed all over and with mud deep up to their knees - while their vehicles had to be rescued later, sometimes days later.

In the most recent attempt, it was the consultant that the district administration had invited to visit the area with a view to submitting an estimate for the rehabilitation work. That team's vehicles also got stuck and they had to walk back to the district headquarters. When their estimate came, it shocked everyone in the district administration who knew that it was almost as much as the total budget for the district programme. They sent it to her anyway, and she had come with her organisation's reply.

"There is no more money," she told them.

Silence.

She waited - these silent pauses could go on for a very long time.

After a while, she continued: "There is a possible solution. We have colleagues in other countries who are experienced in labour-based road rehabilitation methods, and we could invite them to visit the Pachwa Road and give an assessment, if you would like."

More silence.

Then, "That sounds like a good idea," one said. "Let them come."

Six months later, a car drove from Kibaale district headquarters, via the Pachwa Road, to Hoima in three hours, compared to the normal five to six or even seven to eight hours via Kagadi. The news spread quickly, and people came from all over the district "to see this miracle for themselves." Even people who claimed to have no interest in roads came to have a look.

There were other things to be seen, too.

She remembers that as the condition of the road improved, so too was there a wave of other developments along the route: rusty, old, and leaking roofs were replaced by new shining CI sheets; children going to school wore bright new school uniforms and proudly carried new copybooks and schoolbags; women paid school fees for their children; and men pruned and trimmed their coffee trees. New black shiny bicycles, new yellow jerry cans, and new black umbrellas - the three essentials of rural life in those parts - were everywhere to be seen. The umbrellas provided shade from the sun as well as protection from the rain. Traders drove along the Pachwa Road to collect coffee beans and said they were happy to pay higher prices to the farmers because their transport costs were much lower.

She remembers the groups of women with their brightly coloured dresses and big smiles. She remembers how happy they were with the new labour-based methods of road rehabilitation and how happy they were to tell their stories to anyone who asked them why they were out working on the roads.

She remembers some of the women's stories.

Some said that they were sceptical at the beginning and argued that women's burdens were already too high. But when they were asked to dig, the women said that they were willing to try. They said they learned early in life how to dig - it was, after all, women's work to dig the fields - and now for the first time in their lives they were being paid for their work. Their work had a new value, and now they could make more decisions at home too about how to spend household income. Many of those women said that labour-based road rehabilitation was one of the best things that had happened to them.

"Now what would you like to talk about?" she asked the officials.

She remembers the silence.

She waited.

"We want to do more of this," they said.

And they did.

CHAPTER 11

ON THE DARKER SIDE

I t was late in the day and she had one more meeting before she could go home. It had been a busy month, as she almost single-handedly juggled the schedules of three or four consultants who were engaged for the external review. It happened somehow that they had little notice of the deadline by which all these studies and reports should be completed, and she was the only one whose schedule was - or was considered to be - flexible. After all, she had no children in school, like her colleagues, who set other deadlines. Anyway, they were a small team of two or three.

She finished her notes, put one file away, and took out the file for her next meeting.

She liked the ring of this man's name: Hamish Goldie-Scot. It seemed to roll around in her head as she remembered her first meetings with him soon after her arrival in Kampala in 1994.

"You need an engineer gone soft," he told her one day as he briefed her on the results of the study of the condition of the local feeder roads in Kibaale District that he had coordinated for the Ministry of Local Government, where he worked as a Civil Engineering Advisor.

She remembers that of the estimated 600 km of rural roads in Kibaale District, the study found that none was in a maintainable condition - all must be rehabilitated. The study recommends using labour-based methods of rehabilitation.

When Hamish finished his assignment with the Ministry of Local Government in Uganda, he went home to Scotland to undertake a one-year's Masters Course in Theology. She thought this an interesting and unusual choice. She smiled as she wondered about the extent to which he might have "gone soft."

Now, two years later, Hamish was back as an independent external consultant reviewing progress with road rehabilitation as part of her organisation's strategic review. He had just returned from Kibaale District, and she was looking forward to the meeting and to his findings, comments, and recommendations.

She remembers that it wasn't a long meeting; he had his materials well organised, his findings were mostly positive, and his recommendations were clear. He noted the initial difficulties with finding an engineer "gone soft," and he was fascinated by the social and engineering achievements with the Pachwa Road, considering the technical challenges and the scepticism surrounding the lack of experience of labour-based methods.

He had a plane to catch from Entebbe in a couple of hours' time.

As they were putting their papers away at the end of the meeting, there were a few minutes to spare and she asked him about the theology course. She even had the cheek to ask him if and how it was relevant to his engineering or development work.

Hamish was very happy with the course and explained that he had been able to focus his study on the theology of development. Finally, he said, "If nothing else, I'm trying to be a better person."

What a sobering thought at the end of a busy day . . . a busy month! she mused.

The thought of "trying to be a better person" stayed with

her as she packed away her papers, collected her money and ticket from the safe - because now she was going on holiday - checked that she had all she needed in her briefcase, locked the office, and set out for home.

It was around 7:00 p.m. and the evening was still bright with about another half hour before darkness fell. She was still surprised at how quickly darkness fell when they were so close to the equator.

The road was busy and there seemed to be more crazy drivers that evening. Or was it that she was more aware as she thought of "being a better person"?

Being a better person means being a more considerate driver, she thought as she manoeuvred through the busy and chaotic traffic. Every time someone tried to overtake her on the inside or the outside, she thought to herself, *you must be in a bigger hurry than I am, so you can go ahead.* She slowed down for everyone who wanted to cross the road in front of her. She felt relieved when she turned off the main road onto the narrow gravel road that led to her home at the top of Tank Hill.

Her relief was short-lived, for almost immediately after turning onto the narrow road she became aware of a white car behind her and the driver seemed very anxious to overtake her.

Where do you want to go? she wondered. *Or where do you expect me to go?*

The road was very narrow, not wide enough for two cars, and there was a building on the left-hand side, so there wasn't anywhere else for her to go.

She raised her hands from the steering wheel and said out loud, "There is nowhere else I can go" even though there was no one to hear her.

Just as she said this, she reached the end of the building on her left and the road widened a little. She noticed in her rear-view mirror that the driver behind her was signalling very impatiently, and she had the feeling that if she didn't move over the car behind would hit her.

She carefully moved over - she was almost in the ditch - and she tried to watch the two sides of her car as the car behind very slowly began to overtake her. She remembers thinking uneasily that, for one who appeared to be in a dreadful hurry, the driver was now taking his time. Instinctively, she moved her elbow and pressed down the door lock.

The car overtook her and then stopped in the centre of the narrow road.

She didn't notice the doors of the car opening, nor the men getting out, but suddenly she was looking at three machine guns: two were pointing at her head and one was pointing towards the front right-hand wheel. Then she noticed that all the doors of the white car were open.

She raised her hands above her head.

"Get out," she heard a voice say as a machine gun moved beside the driver's door, pointed at her head.

She tried to turn towards the door, but she couldn't - her seat belt held her in place.

"Get out," she heard a nervous voice say.

"I can't," she said, waving her hands that she still held above her head. "I have to open my seat belt and unlock the door."

She doesn't know why but somehow this seemed a safer way to respond, she remembers thinking.

"I'm going to open my seat belt now," she said and moved her right hand while keeping her left hand in the air and her gaze on the machine gun.

It seemed to take forever!

Then she said that she was going to unlock the door. She put her right hand up in the air and moved her left hand to pull up the lock.

She hadn't noticed the other guns move, but now she heard the door behind the driver's seat open.

"Get out," she heard a voice yell at her.

She opened the door and carefully got out.

As she stood at the side of the narrow road beside her car, she could see her briefcase standing on the floor behind the driver's seat - where she had thought it was a safe place to keep it.

She thought of everything she had in her briefcase: reports and papers that could be no use to anybody else, her computer with all her work information, her address book, her diary, her air ticket, and her money.

Her instinct stopped her from stretching out her arm to take it, while at the same time she remembers thinking that she could easily reach it.

"Can I have my briefcase?" she meekly asked, looking at a machine gun. She didn't hear any answer.

Someone climbed into the driver's seat and someone else climbed into the seat behind him, while the third machine gun disappeared into the little white car. She remembers that the engine made a terrible noise before the car drove away.

The road was a cul-de-sac and it was too narrow for the cars to turn.

Her car followed the little white car straight ahead up to the first crossing where both cars turned right. That road was even narrower, and it led nowhere either.

She remembers hearing the roars of the engines, and she imagined the efforts to turn the two cars in the narrow space.

Then the sounds came closer as her car followed the little white car back down the road from Tank Hill.

She met her car driving recklessly as she walked up the hill to her home.

It wasn't far to her home, but mostly what she remembers is, as she walked up the hill, her feet like heavy weights on her legs that now felt like jelly. She wanted to sit down, she wanted to scream, and she wanted help!

She silently walked on and up the hill.

She had her mobile phone in a purse on her belt - the only one of her possessions that wasn't in her briefcase - but she didn't dare take it out and use it. She didn't know why. Her full attention was on moving one foot past the other, on and up.

Trying to be a better person may have saved her from a worse fate that day!

* * * * *

As planned, she had a short break over the Easter holiday, and then it was full steam ahead with the internal review.

The meetings were progressing well, and everyone was happy that senior officials from the relevant ministries travelled to and within the district to review progress. Everyone they met seemed to have a story they wanted to tell about how the new works in the district positively impacted on their livelihoods, and the mood was good.

She also was in good spirits, but her body didn't seem to agree. She was stiff and it was becoming more and more difficult to get out of bed in the mornings and to climb in and out of the cars that were designed for tough conditions rather than for comfort. Despite the progress with road rehabilitation works, travelling was still difficult, and her back seemed to register the bumps as they travelled around.

She tried to ignore these symptoms - thought of them more as irritations than anything else. But one evening, back at the district guesthouse, all preparations were made to have a celebratory dinner with members of the District Council and district administration heads. Her body refused to cooperate. She couldn't find a comfortable position. She tried standing, walking about, sitting on different chairs - with higher or lower seats - but it made no difference. Nothing worked; nothing eased the pain. And she was disturbing others, too. Everybody seemed to become uncomfortable on her behalf as they suggested things she might try to do.

The following day, she rolled out of the bed and propped herself up against the wall as she showered without being able to reach to her feet, and by the time she had dried herself off, she wasn't able to do anything else. She lay back down on the bed.

Later in the day, she was driven back to Kampala, lying on the back seat of the car.

Disk degeneration was the diagnosis, and after nine weeks of lying on her back, she was advised to develop a new lifestyle, beginning with small steps and slowly building up her capacity to walk and work again.

"Pain won't kill you; you just have to learn to live with it," she remembers somebody saying.

* * * * *

Now it was about a year later, on a fine Sunday evening. There were more and more stories of car hijackings in Kampala, some were very violent. For a while, even though she was quite a calm person, she worried about how she might react if she were in such a situation again; she feared that anger could cause her to do something crazy.

But now she was again enjoying her work and her regular exercise routines and relaxation, and she felt quite strong. She particularly enjoyed swimming and massage. She regretted that there weren't many opportunities for walking but didn't dwell on that for long.

She was happy to be a practice case study for aromatherapy. She went for a session that Sunday afternoon as usual and enjoyed a wonderful massage before the weekly film evening at the American Club.

"Do you take the back road these days?" she asked as she prepared to leave for the film.

"Yes, I think it's quite safe at this time of the day," was the reply.

She felt very relaxed but she hadn't decided which road to take; she would decide along the way.

At the first possible turn-off, there were a lot of people around the junction. She turned left onto the gravel road and drove carefully through all the people who easily moved aside to allow her pass.

She was surprised and a little annoyed when she noticed a car behind her that wanted to overtake.

Where do you want to go?, she thought

She quickly surveyed her options, for she was more than a little suspicious.

She chose a point a little further ahead where there were a lot of people, and she moved over to the left and slowed down. The car behind seemed to hesitate but then overtook her, very slowly, and continued slowly up the hill.

That's odd for someone who seemed so anxious to overtake, she thought to herself.

At a T junction a little further ahead, she noted which way the car went: it turned right and then immediately turned left onto the road that she had planned to take over the hill. She decided to change her route.

She turned right at the T junction and continued straight ahead. That road would also take her to the American Club, but the distance was a little longer. The road surface was not as good, so her progress would be slower.

A very short time later, she was horrified to notice in her rear-view mirror that the car was behind her again and this time driving very aggressively.

There were very few people walking on this road so she could not expect that type of protection again. She couldn't increase her speed because of the poor road surface.

The car drove right up behind her and she thought she could see guns.

There were a couple of houses a short distance ahead that afforded the only protection she thought she could find on this road. She decided she would pull over and allow the car to pass.

As soon as she did, she was overtaken, but the car immediately stopped at an angle in front of her, blocking her way. She jammed her foot on the brake and her car slid in the dust but stopped without hitting the car in front.

Then she noticed the machine guns pointed at her.

She calmly opened her door and put her hands in the air.

One moved quickly to the open door.

"Get out," she heard a voice roar at her.

"I'm trying to," she roared back, surprised at the sound of her own voice.

Still looking at the gun, she put her right hand across to open her seat belt as she said: "I have to open this belt first."

She looked away from the gun to click her seat belt open and noticed her little bag lying on the passenger seat. She slowly stretched her left hand over and picked up the bag.

She noticed the gun following the bag as she climbed out of the car but she quickly turned and walked away, back towards the houses.

If I'm going to be shot, I'll be shot in the back, she remembers thinking.

She walked away from her car and the machine guns with her head held high, giving a false impression of confidence. Her knees felt like jelly. She focused on the first house a little distance away and then on moving her feet, one in front of the other, again, and again, and again.

Looking back, she sees all of this in her mind's eye in silent slow motion. She sees someone coming to the front of the house and inviting her to sit down on the low bench - a piece of a fallen tree. She sees someone offering her a glass of water. She hears someone telling her the registration number of the car that stopped her.

She has no memory of hearing her car move away and she didn't look back to see what happened.

Since it was Sunday evening, it took a little time before she made contact with colleagues, who came to help her.

She remembers very little about sitting at the police station, but she has one memory about form filling with a lot of attention paid to her date of birth. She remembers wondering what her date of birth had to do with an armed car hijacking.

The film was almost over when she arrived at the American Club.

A week or two later, she was still feeling angry and frustrated at the helplessness of the car hijacking situation. People told her it was important to work this stress out of her system and to give herself time to do that. Perhaps a holiday would help.

"Mauritius?" she remembers asking, and then answering: "Yes, I'd like to go to Mauritius; I think I'd like to go anywhere."

Everything was soon organised, and they left Kampala on a Saturday morning. They had an overnight stay in Harare and an early flight the following morning.

They had made no reservation for Harare but picked a relatively cheap hotel that colleagues knew of, thinking they wouldn't need to spend much time there. They took a taxi from the airport and had no trouble finding the little hotel where there were rooms free. They were a little surprised when they were asked to pay cash in advance - the hotel didn't take credit cards. They were then shown to their room.

They looked at their watches and decided that if they wanted to do any shopping they should leave immediately, as everything in Harare closed for a half day on Saturdays.

They arrived in town shortly before closing time. They didn't mind this because they hadn't anything in particular they needed to buy. And they had been told that, if at all possible, they should treat themselves to afternoon tea at Meikles, the well-known five-star family hotel.

A short time later, they allowed themselves sink into the luxury of the lounge at Meikles. They joked about the triangular cucumber sandwiches and enjoyed the lightness of the little scones served with homemade strawberry jam and fluffy whipped cream, all washed down with Earl Grey tea.

An hour or so later, they emerged out of the hotel into the

mid-afternoon sun and decided to walk back to their hotel. They sauntered along, still enjoying their moments of grandeur at Meikles. They paused at a four-way junction, checked the traffic in all directions, and crossed over. There wasn't much traffic and not many people either. They sauntered on.

Suddenly, she had a feeling she was choking. She put her hand to her neck and tried to ease the pull on the shoulder strap of her little bag but it tightened instead. She turned her head to catch her breath, and before she knew what was happening, she lost her balance and fell to the ground.

She became aware of being pulled along the ground, back in the direction from which they had come.

Her memories are blurred because everything happened so quickly.

She remembers a voice running along beside her, shouting, "Give that back to me, you little bastard."

She remembers as she lay on the ground seeing a hand catching a grip of the guy's white string vest before those strings disintegrated between the fingers.

She remembers someone running around the corner of the junction they had just crossed over. A wine-coloured car that had no registration number and no maker's sign pulled away from the kerb leaving only a cloud of dust behind.

She was helped up from the ground.

She felt dazed and stiff. She was surprised to see blood running from the fingers of her left hand and slowly realised why. She had held on to her bag so tightly that the strap cut into her fingers as she was pulled along the road.

My bag! she thought. *I've just been mugged, and everything's in that little black bag.*

It took awhile for them to find the police hut where they

were sent to report the mugging incident and the robbery of the little black bag, and an equally long time for the officer to record everything that was in it: her air ticket, passport, credit cards, money, address book, diary, and the key to their hotel room . . . all her important things!

"How could all that fit into what you describe as a little bag?" she remembers the policeman asking.

That was her first small bag - the one she had rescued from the seat of the hijacked car about two weeks earlier!

Back at the hotel, there was no spare key to their room. The housekeeper had the only extra key and she was gone home early because it was Saturday afternoon.

" . . . and because tomorrow is Sunday, she'll come in late," the receptionist told them as he offered them the key to another room and told them they would have to wait for the housekeeper to get access to their bags.

"If you need to stay here for more than one night," the receptionist responded to their questions, "you must pay cash in advance."

It would take at least a week, they discovered, for her to get a new passport, get a new air ticket issued, and get access to money. In the meantime, they couldn't stay at that hotel because they had no more cash!

That left them with only one option: move to Meikles and pay with her friend's credit card.

She remembers standing by the swimming pool on the roof of Meikles Hotel, wondering why her arm, her elbow, her shoulder, and her leg were sore.

"Just go for a swim" she remembers being told.

* * * * *

She heard screams . . . she heard herself screaming, and she remembers that she tried to scream even louder.

This time she had a new colleague drive her home from the office. The traffic was heavy and their progress around the roundabout was slow. She was talking about her visit to South Africa in preparation for a transfer there when they heard the little click of a door opening.

She turned her head and gaped in wonder as a little man took her computer bag from the back seat of the car and limped off into the maze of narrow side streets.

Her colleague pulled the car over onto the path, jumped out leaving his door open, and ran after the little man with the limp.

That was when she heard herself scream.

She didn't know she had this capacity to scream, but this was the last straw.

She had brought the computer into the office that day because there was some problem that she couldn't resolve at home. While in South Africa, she bought a new modem because the old one had been sizzled by a power surge. The new modem needed a special part to complete the installation on her old computer and the people in the computer shop needed to test all the pieces together. They were now all neatly packed in the computer bag that had just disappeared out of sight in the hands of the little man with the limp.

She stopped screaming and waited, as if glued to the seat of the car. She remembers reflecting that this time there was no one telling her to get out.

After what seemed like a very long time, her colleague came back without finding any trace of the little man with the limp or her computer in those small dark streets. She was glad, at least, that he had come back and that she didn't have to go looking for him.

"Maybe," a friend said later, "someone else needs those things more than you do."

"Maybe?" is all she can remember thinking.

Chapter 12

Paradise

She remembers her first visit to Brantevik. It was in the wonderful spring of 2000. She remembers waking up early on her first morning (it was late April) to the sounds of birdsong and the sea. They called her out to join in their morning chorus.

She was soon dressed, and as she put on her walking boots, she was glad she had worn them from South Africa.

She had arrived in Brantevik in the late afternoon and was welcomed with champagne and a look at a map, where she located Brantevik in the southeast corner of Sweden - almost as far southeast as one can go in Sweden and still be on land.

In the evening, her host had served a most wonderful dinner of cod, prepared in his special way, topped with chopped hard-boiled egg, served with boiled potatoes, garnished with parsley and melted butter, and accompanied by a chilled dry and crisp white wine.

She slept well, and now she was out and ready to explore the coastline of the Baltic Sea. She followed the sounds south with the sea to her left, where the track was easy to follow through the fields. The water shimmered in the early morning sunshine and the little waves lapped gently against the rocky shore.

The vegetation changed from field to field. She came to a field that was sheltered on all sides by low bushes and what looked like dead elm trees. At the end of this field, the path curved towards the shore. She stopped and a large rock seemed to beckon to her. She walked over loose stones and sat down on the rock.

Soon she was lost in the beauty, the calm, the freedom.

She allowed the morning sun to massage her face and she reminded herself to breathe in deeply, hold it for a count of ten, and then breathe out again.

Freedom! Oh, wonderful freedom! she mused.

She could almost feel the freedom flowing through her veins, as if her blood had been frozen and was now thawing out in this beautiful sunshine with her feet in the Baltic Sea. She doesn't remember taking her boots off but now she sees that they are safely perched on another rock.

Perhaps I did die and am now in paradise? she wonders.

A couple of weeks earlier, her car had been overturned at a road junction in South Africa. She had just flown from Durban to Johannesburg. It was a fine Sunday evening and dusk was falling as they left the airport motorway to drive into Pretoria, where she lived at that time. She would be home in about ten minutes.

As they approached the junction on the slip road, they slowed down to stop as the traffic light turned to red. But for some reason that she didn't understand at that time, the car (a white Land Rover Discovery) didn't stop; it kept moving forward into the junction, past the red light. She felt a little dizzy.

"What's happening?" she asked her colleague, who was driving.

She looked across and saw the confused look on his face too, and she saw how he was trying to steady the steering wheel.

She can still see all of this happening in slow motion in her mind's eye, but she knows that it happened very fast.

As they moved forward in the junction, the car felt very

unsteady, but she reasoned that they would soon be safely through.

But instead of continuing straight ahead, the car swayed a little from side to side, then veered to the right, toppled over, and continued to spin like a top in the middle of the junction.

What neither of them saw was the car that came behind them at high speed and crashed into them as they prepared to stop. The car drove under their Discovery and powered them forward, unbalanced, until their car toppled over.

She could hear engines roaring, voices calling out, and then another crash.

We must get out of here or we'll be killed, she remembers thinking.

Later she learned that, because this was an accident-prone junction, tow-trucks waited in line for business in the shade of the nearby trees. Having witnessed the accident, one of those tow-trucks drove up beside them to get the business of towing their car away. The crash she heard was that tow-truck being hit by a car travelling through the junction with the green light that otherwise would have hit them as their car spun around.

Meanwhile, as she hung from her seat belt, aware of the sound of their engine as well as the sounds from outside and realising that her arms and legs were too short to reach any tangible objects, she tried to see where her colleague was.

She remembers that her biggest fear then was that their car could catch fire and that they must turn off their engine!

But it was dark now and she couldn't see her colleague.

She heard voices outside come closer, saw more lights. She could see her colleague now, but he didn't answer when she called to him. She heard a woman's voice from outside and then banging on the windscreen. Then she heard another crash and more voices. There were a lot of people outside now.

Someone was trying to open the doors, but the electric locks were jammed.

She felt really helpless, hanging from her seat belt.

Then her colleague started to move, to groan. Slowly at first, he asked what was happening and said he was okay. He became aware of their situation: of her helplessness and of the activity outside. He began to join in. He was a tall man, with long arms and long legs. He was able to reach to the ignition key, and he turned off the engine. With his long legs, he began to kick at the windscreen at the same time as the people outside who were trying to break them free. Soon the windscreen began to crack and people were able to stretch their arms in, break other windows, and open a door.

It took a little longer to release her from her seat belt, and then she was helped to climb over seats and out of the car.

Someone found her glasses in the back of the car, intact, and she remembers being very happy to have them back, to be able to see again.

How strange that I didn't think of my glasses, she remembers thinking afterwards.

She remembers how a young woman hugged her tightly.

She remembers feeling confused as a man asked her if she wanted him to tow her car away while someone else asked her to get into an ambulance - and all the while the warnings about not giving the keys of their car to anyone she didn't know screamed inside her head.

There were many local horror stories about robberies at accident sites.

By now her colleague had quite a bump around the big gash on the side of his forehead just above his right eye. She had tried to telephone other colleagues but without success. They were very few in number and it was Sunday evening.

She remembers that the ambulance driver began to get impatient with her.

"If you don't get into the ambulance and go to the hospital, then I need you to sign this form," she remembers hearing him say while he pushed a paper in front of her.

She remembers wondering what the man was talking about, feeling that she hadn't time to read or to sign anything at that time, as she was trying to figure out what to do about their car. She couldn't go away and leave it lying in the middle of the junction, and she couldn't give the key to a stranger.

What could she do? She felt swamped by feelings of being alone, responsible, and helpless. She was also worried about her colleague with the big bump on his head.

She decided to get into the ambulance and told the man with the tow-truck to take care of their car. He handed her a business card as a receipt.

She seems to remember that there was a third patient in the small ambulance. She couldn't see the third person who seemed to be strapped onto a stretcher and with a brace around the head.

She doesn't remember much about the hospital except bright lights and x-ray machines.

She remembers being discharged from the hospital many hours later, and standing on the steps outside the hospital door, waiting for a taxi to go home.

The next thing she remembers is waking in her own bed with severe pain in her lower back and hip, wondering why, and then remembering the accident. It was 5:00 a.m. the next day.

The next days seemed to bring new pain in other parts of her body along with more x-rays at another fancy hospital but with no results, and finally long sessions with physiotherapists.

* * * * *

She remembers the feel of the grass on her bare feet as she walked back to Brantevik that first morning, and how her boots felt heavy in her hands but there was a new lightness in her step.

She noticed a special sound from the engine of a small fishing boat as it passed south - an unusual sound but soothing in its own rhythmic way.

The birds continued to sing.

Oh, the glorious freedom of walking - and in a beautiful place, too! This must be paradise, she thought to herself, grateful that she didn't have to cancel this, her second visit to Sweden.

* * * * *

Her first visit had been about six months earlier. She came from South Africa then as well to attend a wedding of friends she knew in Uganda in the lovely old university city of Lund.

At the wedding dinner in one of the old university buildings, she was surprised when she couldn't find her name at the table with other friends she knew from Uganda. *Have they forgotten that I'm here?* she wondered.

"Your name is over here," someone said, pointing to a table at the far end of the room.

She ran her eyes down the guest list but didn't recognise any names at that table. *Oh well, I'll just have to make the best of this,* she decided as she went off to find her place at the table. Now she was back in Sweden as the guest of the man who was her dinner companion at that table.

The sun shone brightly in Brantevik every day during that week in late April 2000. What wind there was turned out to be gentle and refreshing, and she felt hypnotised by the ever-changing colours of the Baltic sea.

She walked often, then sat or lay in the garden reading, sharing her chair or blanket with the beautiful Rhodesian ridgeback, Swayo, who had adopted her and didn't leave her side. Sometimes she had to struggle with him to have a piece of the blanket to lie on.

She ate wonderful dinners that her host prepared. And she fell in love.

What can one say about falling in love?

An answer came to her in the form of a memory from Kampala, from that time of year when parents anxiously watched the fax machine at the agreed times for news of exam results. She remembers the anxious waiting, the ringing sound and then the hum of an incoming message.

Those without prearranged times knew to stay away from the fax machine and respected the privacy while pages, rolled from the machine, were anxiously picked up. School reports, exam results, and points were scrutinised until finally the news was ready to be shared.

In the midst of all the pages came one two-line message. She can still see the tears as the message was read aloud:

"There's not much to say about my results, just straight As."

This is my "straight As," she thought.

She walked every day during that first week in Brantevik, alone and with her new friend. She walked because she liked to, because she needed to, and she noticed less pain after each walk. She knew that she was lucky: lucky that her injuries were not more severe; lucky that she could walk; lucky to be alive to enjoy these moments.

She tried not to think about South Africa. But when she did, she had to admit that the accident was not the only issue she must face. She loved her work but not always the politics. The result of compromise, she remembers thinking, is still compromise and the playing fields were seldom equal.

She remembered the many wonderful people she had met and admired in South Africa, but despite this she found the atmosphere and attitudes, in general, to be very difficult. Many people were angry. Some felt that changes were happening too quickly and they were losing too much. Others felt that changes were not happening fast enough as they learned that economic realities could be as powerful as apartheid in preventing them from moving as they wished. Sometimes she felt that she - because she was white - was being held responsible for the system of apartheid and that she must take the consequences.

Reported cases of crime were on the increase. She was warned that it wasn't safe to walk in the lovely parks, even in daylight, because of an increased risk of rape, robbery, or other violence. Everybody was nervous and everybody was suspect, too.

Only two weeks earlier, she had been accused of trying to steal a car! It was after the accident that she had to rent a car because their Discovery had been written-off by the insurance company. She needed to go to Cape Town for meetings, and her secretary agreed to drive her, in the hired car, to and from the airport in Johannesburg, and to take care of the car while she was away. Her driver colleague was unable to work because of his injuries.

A couple of days after she returned to Pretoria and just before she left for Sweden, a group of what she remembers as about six huge people arrived into her office, introducing themselves as police who wanted to talk to her about the hired car. She invited them in and remembers thinking that her little office was very crowded - she remembers that at least one had to stay outside because they couldn't all fit inside her office. She wondered why they were so many?

As they talked about the hired car, she remembers feeling that the atmosphere was a bit aggressive. She listened to and answered questions but couldn't understand the point of their questioning. After a while, she reminded them that they were in a foreign embassy and that if they continued to be so aggressive she would have to get the ambassador to ask them to leave.

They changed tack. She remembers hearing that they were not police but from a security company engaged by the car hire company to investigate an attempted robbery of the rented car. She heard that she was suspected of attempting to sell the car over the weekend.

She stood up to go to call the ambassador to ask them to leave. As she did so, she heard a voice suddenly say that a man had been arrested and charged with the attempted theft and sale of the car while she was away.

This experience was, she thought, relatively minor compared to the armed hijackings and house robberies she had experienced in Uganda. Still it had a deep impact on her.

She remembered when she coordinated arrangements for the then Taoiseach (Irish Prime Minister) Bertie Ahern's visit to Irish Aid programmes in South Africa earlier that year. Most of the small programmes supported by Irish Aid that he visited were crime prevention for youth.

She remembers feeling relieved that in this new freedom in Brantevik she could acknowledge that she felt a great threat of violence in South Africa.

When it was time to leave that wonderful place, Brantevik, she felt renewed in body, mind, and spirit.

Paradise - wonderful to visit! Freedom - wonderful to experience, for a while!

* * * * *

In Dublin, she had a time to visit her doctor. He recommended that she didn't go back to South Africa.

What a shock! But, of course she had to go back – even for six months, as promised. There was so much to do and nobody else to do it; so many people depended on her.

"Okay," her doctor said to her. "Do as you must; it's your life. But if you want your body to heal, don't go back. Healing takes time, and I recommend you give it the time it needs."

But she knew she must go back. She had a ticket booked for one week's time.

During the next week, she prepared herself for travelling; she would go on Sunday as planned. She had decided she would stay for only six months - enough time to recruit a replacement - and then she would let her body heal.

As the week went on, she was more uncomfortable with her decision. She felt more pain in her body and more doubt about how she would be able to continue her work in South Africa, which had probably been the most demanding and least satisfying of her working experiences.

Why do it? she began to ask herself.

On Friday, she telephoned her doctor to say she had decided not to travel back to South Africa. He told her that he thought it would probably be one of the best decisions of her life.

She wondered? She wasn't a big risk taker but she

remembers only a little worry about what would be next?

On that Sunday, at the time when her flight was due to leave - without her - she had a sensation of letting go of a big old coat that she had unknowingly carried around with her for a very long time. In her memory this was a grey tweed coat with many pockets and each one was filled with stones: stones of different sizes, shapes, and colours. The stones had beautiful designs but all were heavy.

What lightness! She remembers thinking.

She was back in paradise.

CHAPTER 13

DREAMING

She could see herself in her dream: she was busy with technologies that she didn't understand; she was trying to fix something. When she woke up, she felt tired as if from physical activity, but she knew what to do with her computer to make it work faster!

Life can be stranger than fiction, she thought.

She wondered about the boundaries between dreams and reality. At one time she thought she could tell, but not anymore - now she wasn't so sure. She had so many dreams that felt real.

There was one dream where she saw her funeral. She saw herself float above the many people as they assembled outside a country church on a fine late summer evening. She heard the birds sing in the trees and the cows low in the fields nearby. She saw the hearse slowly arrive with the coffin that carried her body; she saw the silent tears in the eyes and in the hearts of her family and friends. The music was haunting, and she could feel the outpouring of love in grief. She thought it was one of the most beautiful scenes imagined.

She wasn't upset in the dream, and she wanted everyone to know that. She wanted to console all the people who grieved, and she wanted them to know that she was okay. "Don't be upset; I've learned something wonderful," she cried out, but she knew that nobody could hear her, nobody could see her. She understood that this vision was a one-way stream.

As she hovered above the crowd, she could see another group of people. They were a little distance away to her right and a little higher up. They were waiting for her. She knew she wanted to go to them but not yet. She wanted to tell her family and friends something: she wanted them to understand that when they knew what she now knew, they wouldn't be upset either.

When she remembers, she doesn't know what it was that she knew, but she knows that it was very important and she can still feel its comfort.

Then she remembers seeing a woman come to the head of the group above her - a woman dressed in a dark suit and a white blouse with a crisp collar. She recognised her: she was her father's cousin, who now opened her arms wide to welcome her to her new home. The welcome was so strong that she floated towards her and into her warm embrace.

In another dream, she's with her sister. They're being shown around a large building - a school or conference centre - and introduced to the activities of each room, all to do with different aspects of death and dying. Again, surprisingly, it is not difficult. The building is bright and colourful, with a lot of glass, especially along the corridor that runs the length of the building. To one side are doors to the classrooms, and outside the windows on the other side is a lovely mature garden. The place is populated with happy people who move from room to room, from presentation to presentation. The overall feel of the place is welcoming and liberating.

She and her sister are gently guided through the process. They can take part in any of the presentations as and when they choose.

Finally, they come to a one-way glass door. It is clearly explained to them that this is the only door from which there is no return. She thought she was ready to go through it and is surprised when she finds herself walking past the door and saying to an assistant, "No, not yet; thank you."

She continues walking with a light heart and turns to say something to her sister. "Oh, my god!" she gasps as she sees her sister go through the one-way door. "This can't be," she says to everyone but no one in particular. "If anyone is to go through that door, it should be me; there is no one depending on me."

Then she calls after her sister: "What is going to happen to your husband and small children? This is a big mistake. Come back. Come back before the door closes."

As she says this, she sees the door closing.

When she woke up from that dream, her pillow was wet from her tears. She stood under the shower for a long time the next morning and then slowly picked up the telephone and dialled her sister's number. The telephone fell out of her hand when she heard her sister's voice.

She remembers a dream where she's swimming in a beautiful turquoise lake at the bottom of an old disused limestone quarry. The sun is just rising above the rim of the limestone, the air is fresh with a promise of heat, and a bird is singing as if it too is enjoying the magical morning. The water is warm. She likes to swim here, especially at this time of day. She comes here as often as she can, sometimes daily.

This day she notices something different: as she swims towards the centre of the lake, the temperature changes and the water seems heavier somehow. She brings her attention back from the birdsong to her swimming. She can't remember having difficulty like this before.

As she focuses on the water, it seems to get heavier and colder. She increases her pressure, pushing herself on. The water is turning black and is becoming sticky, like tar. She can't smell anything different, but she can definitely feel it. She is getting tired. It is now very difficult to move her arms and legs in the thick heavy substance.

I must get out of here, get away from this tar! she thinks frantically.

She tries to turn. It's difficult and slow.

"Concentrate," she tells herself. "Lift your right arm and swing it over your head, lift your left arm and swing it over your head, and remember to kick your legs."

She continues in this way, so concentrated on moving her arms and legs that she has no idea how much time has passed.

When she hears the bird singing again, she knows that she's safe, and then she notices that the water is lighter and warmer, like it usually is, and she can breathe easily again. She continues swimming towards the edge of the lake.

She wonders if she has been dreaming - should she try swimming towards the centre again? She decides she must; otherwise, she'll never know.

She turns and swims towards the centre. She has only gone a short distance when it all starts again.

"I have to get out of here," she knows. "Otherwise, I'll be lost forever."

The alarm clock rang, and as she stretched over to switch it off, she felt a strain in her arms, as if she had been training hard.

She also knew that she didn't need to worry about choices or decisions that she soon had to make in real life; she knew that all would be as it should be.

CHAPTER 14

ANOTHER RAINBOW

S he sees herself standing beneath a waterfall. She hears the roar of the water. She sees the individual drops of water that separate from the great mass of the river as they spray over the falls. She marvels at how they dance and play in the sunlight, creating a rainbow.

She is almost hypnotized as she watches the drops of water as they tumble down and rejoin the river as it continues on its long journey through Africa. She has no words to describe the sense of loss and gain she feels as the drops of water disappear without a trace, as they lose their individuality and swell the great river.

Perhaps it is simply balance? she thinks.

She notices as individual stories disappear and swell the waves of memories that tumble over her, they create their own balance.

There is a new waves of memories and these are from Cambodia.

"You should think about Cambodia", the Big Man said to her one day in late 2001, and then he continued: "There may be some work there that needs your attention and your skills".

She wasn't prepared for this. After all, he was retired and had no direct involvement in that work anymore, and she had just spent two years allowing her body to heal and her new life to develop by the Baltic Sea.

She remembered the day the physiotherapist recommended that her best treatment from now on would be regular walking. She remembers feeling very grateful because she knew that she would be able to walk while, despite good intentions, other types of exercise would simply be more difficult for her to pursue.

"Walking", she said to herself, "in this wonderful place, with this wonderful man, is something I most surely will do, every day, for as long as I can".

Now she was enjoying her new energy, flexibility, and fitness.

She was initially shocked as she listened to the Big Man's suggestion; she thought she had finished with that work, and she wondered how she could leave this beautiful place. The Big Man didn't say much; he didn't need to say much. He had seeded an idea that soon began to grow into a plan.

A couple of months later, she moved with her husband and their dog to Cambodia on a three-year assignment.

Their dog, a Rhodesian Ridgeback, was a minor celebrity. He was named Swayo after one of the Ridgebacks in Laurens van der Post's *A Story Like the Wind*, and Swayo's grandfather had starred in the film version of that story. He was big--some said he was as big as a sheep or a small calf.

She remembers the energy of Phnom Penh, a city with a very young population, a very young average age. She remembers the joy they experienced during their early morning walks in the busy Monument Park as they joined in the city's early morning exercise routines, and also as they travelled by cyclo and chatted with children going to and from school.

She remembers thinking that everyone in the city must be going to school: children went in two shifts, from 6:00 a.m. 12.00 p.m. and from 12.00 p.m. 6:00 p.m., and then adults went from 5:00 p.m. to 9:00 p.m. after they finished their day's work, and at week-ends. She remembers that there seemed to be a great hunger for education, a hunger to make up for lost time under the Khmer Rouge when education was not permitted.

She remembers the little scooters that carried whole families: father, mother, two or three children, their pets, their shopping, and their furniture.

She remembers sitting upstairs in the FCC, eating the King Prawn Noodles that her husband loved, and watching the flow of the great Tonle Sap River that changed direction every year at the beginning and at the end of the rainy season, and learning that the livelihoods of millions of people and the abundance of the Tonle Sap Lake depended on that change.

She remembers the empowering effect of teamwork displayed by her co-workers after the staff from three individual programmes worked together with local communities to study the dynamics and impact of two years of successive flooding, the shock in their eyes when they reported their conclusion that long established practices were now inappropriate, and the liberating effect of changing them.

She remembers the shock, horror, and fear, in a voice over the telephone reporting to her the discovery of corruption.

She remembers another liberating shock--and it happened around the same time--when staff in other project areas acknowledged that good intentions did not automatically lead to good outcomes, and how tears flowed as she was thanked, for what was described "opening a window and letting fresh air blow through".

She remembers how, as she developed relationships, people told her stories.

She remembers a story about a brave four-year-old who was arrested by Khmer Rouge officers and paraded naked through a camp because she/he had dared to go into the rice field and "steal" and eat rice that had not yet ripened because she/he was so hungry.

She remembers a story of children who had only a mosquito net to use as a shroud to wrap the body of a mother, and their grief at learning that the body had been removed and buried in an unknown place while they went to seek help.

She remembers hearing of the enthusiasm of young people in a refugee camp who had jobs caring at night for a couple of pigs, for which they received extra food rations. But more importantly, she remembers the joy in the story at the freedom to choose different courses to attend in the camp schools--all day long, every day. She remembers the feeling that the hunger for learning rather than food would never be satisfied.

She remembers a story of a young woman who would marry the man who would solve the complicated puzzle that she and her sisters had created as a way of selecting a good husband.

She remembers the pride in the faces of people who carried their tattered and torn village CLTS (Community Led Total Sanitation) maps with them for years. In the time she knew them, they never lost their eagerness to explain the progress of CLTS in their villages, illustrated on the maps as the communities changed the colour from red (Open Defecation) to green (Open Defecation Free).

She remembers sitting in a village as people calculated the change in the average household daily income over the two years since they adopted CLTS and declared their village Open Defecation Free (ODF). According to thier calculations, they declared that they had worked their way out of poverty with a new average daily income of about two U.S. dollars a day.

She remembers the story of a young woman who described her first visit to Phnom Penh--her first visit to a big city. She was fascinated by so many people, so much traffic, so much noise, so many lights, so many different smells. She wanted to stay up all night to savour and prolong the experiences. But she couldn't, as she had to get up early the next morning and be ready to make her first ever presentation to a large crowd of people about her successful micro business. She was a finalist in the first Cambodian Microfinance Awards.

Microfinance! A storm of memories build as she remembers the paradox of the savings and credit programme.

Paradox! She wonders why? . . . She used to ask *why* about many things, but not so often any more since she made a determined effort to stop asking *why*. But she allows herself an occasional lapse.

She remembers wondering why people used the language of pregnancy, childbirth, and motherhood when they spoke about the savings and credit programme.

She remembers that it was never intended that she be the director of that programme; how she was assured at her appointment that she wouldn't have anything to do with it. She remembers the explanation that the programme had been voluntarily registered with the National Bank of Cambodia (NBCA) a couple of months before her arrival and therefore must, according to the new Cambodian law, be transformed into a Cambodian Microfinance Institution within one year of registration. The task was great enough that a dedicated director position had been created to manage the transformation.

She remembers that difficulties with the programme were many and had been well documented before she arrived on the scene. She remembers her surprise at reading a report wherein it was described as a runaway train at the top of a steep hill.

She remembers learning that there was no blueprint for

success, and how decisions taken were proving difficult to activate.

She remembers that a complication for her was that she was responsible for that programme until the new director arrived, and she was reminded often that she would be held accountable in Cambodia for compliance with the new law.

She rememebers that it was not a high priority programme for her organisation. Some thought that it was taking up too much time and resources. Some worried that it was or must move away from the organisation's stated target group of the poorest of the poor--a move known as "mission drift" within the industry--and that this lessened its priority even further.

She remembers how supporters, most of whom she never met, talked or wrote about the programme as a premature baby. Its survival thus far was thanks to the remarkable achievements of dedicated people within the limited resources available to them. But they were aware that, because of natural growth, the programme had already exceeded the capacity of those limited resources to work effectively or effeciently. They argued that, like all premature babies, it needed support.

She remembers wondering why the people with experience whom her organisation wanted to employ to manage the transformation wouldn't take the new job. Later, she thought she understood why, and it was a hard-earned realisation. When she had already completed the work and understood the extent and scale of the difficulties, she concluded that managing the transformation from an NGO programme into a Microfinance Institution in such uncertain circumstances was something that would not voluntarily be undertaken twice in a lifetime!

She remembers the slow, painful realisation that nobody else was going to take on the task, while at the same time she learned that the livelihoods of poor people were being affected by the delays. This became the catalyst for her to act. She was, after all, by nature a "fixer"; she really had no choice.

In the early days, she remembers, it often seemed like she had walked into a twlight zone of indecision wherein the premature baby did not stop growing. Rather, it started growing into a monster.

She remembers how she reluctantly became a supporter of the monster and, like other supporters, she began thinking and talking about it as a premature baby. She remembers thinking that it should either be allowed to die with dignity or be supported to develop into a healthy baby. She didn't mind which, but she understood that a decision was necessary. She couldn't get a decision to allow the premature baby to die with dignity. Therefore, it became her priority not only to save and protect the monster but to find a way to release and tame it.

She remembers that she knew it was risky. But why it should be so risky, she didn't know and still doesn't understand.

"Risking success", she remembers a young voice saying to her.

Focus on what needs to be done, she told herself for months, for three years. She did, and in the process a new Microfinance Institution, AMK, was born.

She remembers writing the principles upon which the new institution should be established. Every time she reads about a new achievement of AMK, a new success, her heart swells with pride, knowing how important those principles proved to be for managing its social performance – the aspect and dimension of the change that worried the "mission drift" people, the most.

She remembers the paper on advocacy that she was asked

to comment on. She remembers its recommendation that issues to be advocated on should be identified through good quality research. This, she thought, could serve her well, too. She remembers thinking that good quality research in this programme, this transformation, would pave the way for whatever would be said about the new institution in the future to be based on well-researched fact rather than on subjective fear, speculation, or opinion.

She remembers the CV that was left on her desk one day just before lunch, along with the comment: "She may be able to help you answer some of your questions; help you with research".

She remembers this as an important milestone on the rocky road to success.

The memory storm darkens, and in the heavy mist that blows in she hears a voice saying: "I don't like the way you talk to me" and again: "I don't like the way you take your holidays".

She feels a lightness in her spirit as the mist clears.

She remembers that some called her the midwife who oversaw the birth of a healthy institution that has become a leader in Cambodia and a winner internationally. She wonders, as she acknowledges that she knows next to nothing about what midwives actually do!

She sees herself more as a surrogate mother who took on a premature baby that was a monster in a maze; one that many had an opinion about but none could tame.

The storm abates.

She remembers the voices of appreciation within the new institution. She remembers the meeting where the work was likened to that of a Cambodian-style relay game wherein the important stick is a pencil. She didn't begin the work and she didn't end it. In her round she played a defining role in getting the new institution started. She found a way to release and tame the monster. She remembers her joy when people assured her that following her example, they "wouldn't lose the pencil".

She remembers that it was at a funeral that she learned about the maturing of her "baby"; about how the new institution had been sold, returning to its former owner one and a half times what had been invested in the institution over the years, and that the first CEO, whom she helped to recruit, would again be involved in its management and governance. She couldn't have wished for a better outcome.

* * * * *

A sunflower blossomed in their Brantevik garden in 2009. They didn't plant it--for a long time they didn't know what it was--and in a most unlikely and exposed place, it survived both the wind and her determined weeding.

For months they watched in silent amazement as it grew tall and strong. When the head began to grow, it turned to face the rising sun. Very slowly, the petals opened and they knew what it was.

On a sunny day in early October, its head was fully grown and the yellow seeds radiated in the green leaves, bowing to the Earth's rotational force.

The circle was complete.

* * * * *

They said farewell to an old suitcase that day. It had been a loyal travelling companion with her over several decades and with both of them over the past decade. It lost a wheel in Copenhagen a couple of years earlier, and on returning to

Cambodia, it had a new one fitted. That helped for a while, for a few more journeys, but it became more difficult and as time went on it seemed to protest more and more, as if it were trying to say: "It's time to let go, time to say farewell".

"What's in that bag?" she asked, just before they put it in the car to take it to their local recycling station.

"Nothing", he replied.

"I'd like to have one last look", she said.

He passed the bag over to her and she opened it.

Inside were two broken straps and the maker's ten-year guarantee.

* * * * *

The sun begins to shine through the broken clouds and she sees these memories in the final act of a great play in which she was given a leading part. She sees herself as one of those tiny drops of water that separates from the great mass, plays and dances in the sunlight and helps to create a rainbow. She sees the wonder as the drops of water rejoin the river and disappear without trace. She understands that there will be another rainbow.

Lightning Source UK Ltd.
Milton Keynes UK
UKOW040600191212

203863UK00002B/3/P